MY SHARE OF THE BODY

My Share of the Body

STORIES

Devon Capizzi

Published by Split/Lip Press
6710 S. 87th St.
Ralston, NE 68127
www.splitlippress.com

ISBN: 978-1-952897-20-7

Cover and Book Design: David Wojciechowski

Editing: Pedro Ramírez

To Ernie, for cracking me open

CONTENTS

"So it could happen: by writing about someone lost—or even just talking too much about them—you might be burying them for good."

—Sigrid Nunez, *The Friend*

MY SHARE OF THE BODY

The urn is small as an egg and fits nicely in the hand. Heavy, weighted. Avery picks it up and shakes it a little. Bits and pieces rattle inside. It's like a shaker from an early music class, but there's something harder too. "You think it's his bones?" Avery's brother Teddy asks, his skin ghost-white and papery as he clutches his own small egg of ashes. Avery shrugs because she doesn't want to say, "I do." Doesn't want the sound of her own voice corrupting the sound of bone in its eternal casing. *So small*, Avery thinks, turning the urn in her hand and wondering how much of him they fit inside.

For weeks, Avery carries the urn wherever she goes. The grocery store has been the same since childhood. A county dairy farm with house-made chocolate milk, and ice cream, and an assortment of local meats and cheeses. Avery throws in a packet of gum after picking up a bag of flour for her mother, who is baking biscuits for her stress.

The cashier, Avery notices, is not much younger than she is. Nineteen now and feeling ancient with dark circles underneath her eyes, taking a break from school, Avery watches the boy scan and bag her groceries. He looks his age. Gangly limbs and teenage acne. The mop of hair and slick of oil on his forehead. Avery is distracted by him only briefly, his life of girl crushes and hand-me-down cars and too-big suits at high school prom. The weight of the urn in her pocket grows heavier, and Avery can feel it in her knees and in her feet. Like she's merging with the glossed linoleum floors. She reaches out and grabs a plastic canister of Tic Tacs. *Maybe*, she muses, *I got a piece of his mouth.*

At the gas station, Avery buys lottery tickets and scratchies. At home, Avery gives her mother the flour and her mother accepts it with empty eyes and nimble fingers. On the countertop, there's a peanut butter and jelly sandwich—half eaten—the only thing Avery's mother has been able to keep down since the accident. Avery doesn't like to think about the sandwiches. As if her mother is nothing but a child again, no kind of mother at all, as if the death of a husband can slap you so hard you lose your mind and body, and what is a mother without a body?

In her bedroom, Avery takes the sharper curve of the urn's flat bottom to scratch the lottery tickets and wins a free coffee from the gas station. Methodically, she takes the tickets she has gifted to the urn. She scratches. The urn upstages her and wins fifteen dollars from the Commonwealth of Pennsylvania. On her bedside table, Avery places the urn so carefully it is almost too intentional. An altar, she considers. But no, her father always warned her, *Never give yourself to something that can't give back.*

On Thursdays, Avery goes to the movies in the afternoon. Her mother has started inviting guests for coffee most days, and Avery can't stand the empty chatter of their voices, of her mother's voice.

More and more, Avery thinks of exposing the urn to others. Considers resting him on the ticket counter. The concession stand, so full of salt and butter the air stings her nose. She buys a bucket of popcorn and knows she'll eat the whole thing, because she is gluttonous. A teenager, again, behind the ticket window. Avery clutches the urn so tightly in her pocket she warms the metal. She thinks, *What pieces are inside of you?* Accepts the movie tickets. Falls asleep in the cool, dark theatre. When she wakes up, she is comforted again to find the urn tucked in her pocket. As much as she wants to share him, the satisfaction lies in keeping him, over and over, to herself.

Back home, her mother won't stop crying in the living room.

Back home, a whole chicken, roasted to perfection for their dinner.

Back home, Avery eats alone. She listens.

Wind through forest trees. The whisper of a distant wind chime. The rustle of dead autumn leaves as they scrape along the patio. Her mother's breathing. The clatter of Avery's knife and fork across plate. The egg inside her pocket. Avery listens for it, but hears nothing.

When she is finished eating, she stays seated at the kitchen table. Exhausted, her shoulders ache. She thinks of Teddy. Big brother. Big belly. Big beard. Big heart. An experiment of his from years ago, *Do you know you can squeeze an egg as hard as you possibly can, and it won't ever break?* When he tried, the egg splattered in his face and the whites clung sloppily to his beard and Avery laughed so hard she snorted orange juice through her nose and she can almost feel it burning now.

She squeezes her egg of ashes. She squeezes it tighter.

On Christmas day, they gather at the family house. They drink eggnog and watch Claymation classics, one foot in front of the other. Teddy eats too much and agrees to stay the night. Avery's mother doesn't eat enough and falls asleep at five p.m. Avery drinks too much and tries to pop the top off of the urn to see inside.

Late at night, alone in her bedroom. Her stupid fingers work the pointed top of it and she questions if it's glued. The space, lit softly by electric candles Avery's mother puts in each window of the house for holidays. Old posters on the wall, peeling at the edges. The face of Juno from *Juno* pouts at her and Avery says, "What?"

She feels the wine in her stomach and in her temples, and *ba-dum-ba-dum-ba-dum*, it beats like blood. She lays back on her twin-sized bed and wonders if she got a piece of his eye when they divvied up the ashes. Avery wonders if she got a piece of his thin-rimmed glasses. Wonders at the picture of him on her bedroom dresser. Years ago, at Disney World. Looking miserable. His forehead sweaty. His belly hugged so tightly by a fanny pack. Avery wonders what's inside the fanny pack. She wonders if they burned him up naked. She falls asleep.

By Easter, Avery's mother has lost so much weight she looks ill. Avery watches her closely, makes sure she fills her plate. Her mother has made lamb and Avery imagines her father's mouth inside the urn inside her pocket. Lamb, his favorite, extra rare, borderline raw. Avery's mother cooks it a sensible medium-well and they eat it with globs of mint jelly in front of the television.

When night falls, Teddy shows up with a coconut cake that looks like a rabbit and Avery has two slices and Teddy falls asleep on the couch again and Avery helps her mother with the dishes.

"I'll wash, you dry," her mother says.

And so, they stand. Shoulder to shoulder at the kitchen sink, Avery watches her mother's hands closely. The arthritic knuckles from her pottery. The dry skin from her pottery. The thin crescent scar from Avery back when she was three years old and tried to cut the strawberries herself, flung the knife around. *Don't be so stubborn* her mother said, annoyed. But Avery wouldn't let it go, remembers that soft, easy feeling of the knife slipping through her mother's skin and feels her belly turn and turn too slowly; she feels dizzy at the thought of blood. She wonders, for the first time maybe, how much her father bled before he died.

"You okay?" her mother asks, her hands still working, the water still warm and sudsy.

Avery nods, takes a plate and dries it off. Takes a bowl and dries it. Takes a spoon, a sharp, serrated knife, a wooden salad prong. They find a rhythm with each other. *I'll wash, you dry*. Avery is struck by the thought that she is standing in her father's place. His feet right where her feet are, and his arms in constant motion. The damp feeling of the dishcloth; he knew this, too. The urn is tucked safely in her pocket. That old, familiar weight.

After, like she is a child again, Avery crawls into her mother's bed and sleeps there next to her. In the middle of the night, she wakes up restless. Underneath her pillow, she finds an old T-shirt that belonged to her father. She replaces it quickly. Turns on her side. Traces the contours of her mother's sleeping face with just her eyes, roaming over sharp nose and thin, crisp lips and new wrinkles at the edges of her eyes. *Crow's feet*, Avery whispers. Her mother snores.

Avery turns on her back and gazes at the empty ceiling. As she falls back to sleep, she thinks about the morning. The angle of the sun, light pouring through the windows, and she wonders if her presence will startle, if her mother might, for one brief and sleepy moment, mistake her daughter's body for his.

Summer is hot and sticky. It smells of dust and dirt and baked manure. Avery wants to peel her skin off, strip herself of sweat and stink and the treetop smell of living in the woods. She goes on hikes, swims in the river. She sees so many young people around it makes her want to die. They float on inner tubes. They drink too much beer.

At home, her mother lives in a one-piece bathing suit and eats nothing but fruit salad with too much pineapple in it. She looks refreshed. She says she started painting again. Avery asks to see her work, but her mother shrugs it off, pretending not to hear, disappears into her studio.

Teddy is seeing a woman again. He says that he's in love and starts doing things he's never done before. Mainly hiking, camping, and yoga. *What is she, a fucking hippie?* Avery says over the phone one afternoon. Teddy laughs, but says nothing. Avery asks when they can meet her. Teddy says he has to go. They're packing for the Poconos.

The urn. Avery has not forgotten about the urn. She has, several times, washed it in the cool creek behind the barn. Once, she took it swimming in the river, but learned her lesson when it slipped from her pruned fingers and she had to spend fifteen minutes looking for it. She found it, hidden among the rocks, all of them like chicken eggs and duck eggs, all of them so heavy.

It's the middle of the night and she can't find him. He used to be right there on the bedside table, underneath the picture of his predecessor. Disney's Magic Kingdom. Again, an accidental altar, or a necessary one. Avery isn't sure anymore. The urn is gone, gone from her pillows and pillowcases, the slippers next to the bed; she checks their cavities.

Finally, she moves the nightstand away from the wall and there he is like a child lost and found inside the grocery store. Avery leans down over the table and can only reach him with her fingertips. The room is dark, but her eyes are adjusted to the dark. And she can see each shadow, each silver stroke of moonlight on her dresser and the patch of hardwood floor, so cold on her bare feet. The bed, ransacked and dismantled. Avery is careful to sit in the very middle. She clutches the urn close to her heart like a precious animal, a baby chick, a guinea pig. She shakes, shakes the urn right next to her ear and she can hear her father's bones as they turn and clatter in their canister. Like the distant noise of heavy rain on metal.

Teddy says he's getting married and moves in with the Hippie. Avery's mother thinks it's good for him, to be in love. She's been in her studio all summer long painting God knows what and Avery's sick of it. *Why won't you let me see it?* she asks. Her mother chews her pineapple, pops a blueberry, says it isn't ready yet. Retreats into her cave.

Avery notices the urn is moving constantly. She finds it on her bedside table. She finds it in the kitchen on the windowsill in godly sunlight. She finds in in her laundry hamper. She finds it in her pocket where it ought to be. *Heavy, heavy*, she whispers to herself.

The workers at the movie theatre know her now. Every Thursday afternoon. Almost a year. Every week, a movie. A bucket of popcorn. The cool, dark theatre, extra satisfying in the summer. It is the only time she sleeps, really sleeps. At home, at night, she stalks the hallways like a bitter ghost. Restless, angry, but she can't remember who she's angry at. She stays up to two a.m. eating sliced turkey sandwiches on potato rolls and watching *Chopped*. In the morning, she finds the urn in the refrigerator. Next to the milk.

August comes. One month. One month until Avery will go back to school and resume a normal life and think of things like *Let's suppose the force that the sun exerts on Mars is exactly 10^{22} Newtons. What would the force be if Mars were twice as far away?* A college sophomore now, she is studying the sky, because she thinks that it's romantic.

Celestial. Avery holds the word in her mouth one afternoon out on the patio. It's too hot, but the umbrella is covered in spider webs and spiders. Avery bakes. She fiddles with the urn in her hand and the metal is warm and tacky with humidity. She looks up at the sky, and she allows herself to imagine something other than the body. Something more, maybe, than a tin of ash and bone. She read online that they don't even get it all when they burn you up. There is no way to harvest all of the remains from the machine.

Her mother is out this afternoon with friends. Avery pictures them in sunglasses. Iced tea and Caesar salads. She turns the urn again, and it reflects harsh sunlight. A laser beam of light falls on the door of her mother's studio and it's decided. Avery gets up and goes inside.

The space is dark and warm. The walls unfinished, lacking drywall and plumes of insulation and there are so many canvases, some small as the cover of a cookbook, some of them taller than Avery and wider than the front grill of a pickup truck. Some of them are facing out–a painting of Lilly pads, a landscape of a nearby Amish farm–some of them are turned to face the wall like they're ashamed. Avery's footsteps are too loud, even though they're quiet.

Like pornography, she knows it when she sees it.

The painting is not him. But it is not, not him. The canvas is textured and black, with hues of purple, gray, and limestone green. There is movement. Streaks of paint across the middle. Nothing is symmetrical. But there is a gradient; light around the edges, darker in the middle.

And it is not his face. There is no face. No body. No recognizable shape, human or otherwise.

And still, he is there somehow. Like when people look at Rothko paintings, just three big blocks of color, and wind up seeing God.

Dinner on the patio. Her last night at home before going back to school. Teddy brings the Hippie and potato salad, Avery's favorite. And Avery's mother makes grilled chicken, grilled zucchini, discs of eggplant, everything charred and salted to perfection. The evening is cool and the Hippie cracks open a beer. Avery has to admit, she loves the Hippie, too.

As the sun dips low, fireflies circle them, blinking yellow light. Teddy looks happy. He's lost weight from all that yoga. The Hippie wipes his chin with her own napkin when oil drips from his mouth.

Avery's mother is eating well again. Her plate looks heavy with the cookout and she sips a bottle of Rosé, chilled and sweating condensation.

Everything is good now. The weather, the food.

Avery eats until she can't eat anymore, leans back. Listens to the chatter of the table. Her mother laughs at something the Hippie says. Teddy is radiant with luck and joy.

When Avery looks over, she is surprised to see her father's chair is empty. And the second jolt—how can she still expect to see him there? Her mother is telling a story from art school, one they've heard a million times about a raccoon in the studio, a garbage exhibition, the stink of trash all through the building. Avery listens, touches each of her pockets in turn before she remembers. The urn is inside on top of her dresser.

Her mother's studio has dirt floors. Avery rolls the urn in the palm of her hand. It is almost ordinary now. Almost like this is nothing but a music shaker, a stress ball, a Pinky ball from childhood.

The painting hasn't changed since Avery first looked at it, and she wonders what her mother does all day, holed up in this old shack. Maybe all she does is stare at it; Avery doesn't blame her.

The floor is harder than she imagined. Rocky and compacted by so many years of her mother's feet treading back and forth and back and forth. Avery's arm is tired, and she lets the shovel fall. She looks at the urn and sees a lot of things.

Movie tickets, popcorn, duck-egg rocks in the river, pocket fuzz and orange Tic Tacs, and laser beams of light and moonlight and bedside tables and fanny packs and Disney World. She tries, again, to pop the top off but can't do it. Thinks that, maybe, she really doesn't want to do it, that her body is protecting itself. That her body won't let her crack it open. That she knows already what's inside; dust, bone.

Avery squeezes her egg of ashes, squeezes tighter. Drops it in the divot in the floor. Covers him with dirt and soot. Covers him like flower seeds and plant seeds and other things that grow. Does so carefully and gently, like he is something sacred. Presses her fingers down, hard into the ground. Leaves her fingerprints all over it. Looks back up and sees his face trapped in the ether.

A YOUNG AND LONELY SUMMER

The summer he killed the bird was the hottest one Mason had ever felt. Michael had been dating his mother for three years by then, the two of them like a couple of teenagers in a movie, at once boring and intriguing. They did everything full-throttle.

Week-long fights. Long bouts of innuendo, grabbing at each other in the middle of the afternoon. When Michael lost his job that summer, he found another fixing cars with a cousin in Virginia. Mason overheard them planning from his bedroom through paper thin walls. His mother's high whisper, so excited. They were going with him. They were moving to Virginia. Mason had turned on his side in his own small bed and the slats creaked at his weight. She hadn't even asked.

They drove the old station wagon, and the car smelled of sweat and leather and tobacco. Mason's baby sister Anna wailed the whole way down, and Mason's whole body felt tired for her as they snaked through wide fields, overgrown with hazy grasses.

The lawn outside their new home was lush and unruly, and the house itself was bookended by two spindly trees, their branches kissing in the middle. Outside, Michael's cousin Steven sat in a vinyl folding chair smoking. They parked the car by the curb, which was not a curb at all, but just the ending of the yard and the beginning of the gravel road. Michael hopped out.

"Hey, you."

Mason looked up. His mother had turned around in her seat, her cheeks flushed with summer. Her skin glistened.

"Be good," she said.

"I am good."

"You know what I mean. You been kickin' his seat the whole way down. I see you."

"I'm hot," Mason said.

"We're all hot. You're nearly thirteen now. You behave yourself."

"You're one to talk," Mason muttered.

When he looked at her again, he could see the sting in her eyes.

"Grab your sister. We're bein' rude," she said, tone clipped as manicured hedges.

Anna was sleeping now, and Mason dreaded waking her. Carefully he reached out and unlatched the buckles on her car seat and she shifted a little and opened her eyes and looked at him.

"What do you think about this?" he said softly. "Nothing, right? Just a baby."

Anna reached her arm out to stretch, and her damp fingers touched Mason's nose as if to comfort him. He smiled and kissed her.

The house was cramped and smelled like dust and cigarette smoke. The floors dipped underneath the carpet when Mason stepped inside. In preparation for their arrival, Steven had separated the spare bedroom into two sections by rigging a sheet to hang from the middle of the ceiling.

"There you go, boy," he said, patting Mason so hard on the back his knees nearly buckled. "I made your own room and all."

Steven looked proud, and Mason resented that look. He stood on his side of the sheet, took a big breath and blew so the sheet billowed out concave. Steven's face fell, his missing canine tooth and the dirt and motor oil worked underneath his fingernails. Mason thought he looked clumsy, like he was too big for himself.

After dinner that night, Mason snuck back through the hallway and shut the bedroom door. The room was small, even without the sheet parsing it in two. But now, he was grateful for the privacy and felt guilty for making a fuss.

On his side of the sheet, a twin-sized mattress rested on the floor beneath the window. Mason sunk his knees into it and looked out.

The back yard had a drying line full of pillow cases, silhouetted now against the sky, which was still light but getting darker. In between the pillow cases, Mason could see into the house next door. A boy about his age was standing taller than he should have at the kitchen sink, probably propped up on a stool. He had blond hair buzzed down almost to his head and he was wearing a pair of oversized yellow kitchen gloves that made his arms look like sticks. A woman Mason took to be the boy's mother stood next to him and passed him dirty dishes one by one. The boy scrubbed each one clean. His collar bones were prominent in his sleeveless undershirt. His skin was tan.

Mason got tired of watching. He stretched out on his mattress and looked up at the ceiling and the shadow of the curtains stretched out long and dark. His stomach felt heavy with dinner and he imagined everything else around it floating to the surface of his skin, like a bunch of empty bottles in a swimming pool.

He fell asleep quickly that first night, waking much later in the cool, dark quiet of well past midnight. A timeless hour. And for no particular reason, he thought of the boy he had seen doing dishes.

In the morning, Steven made buttermilk pancakes. Strong coffee and bacon. Mason shuffled into the kitchen, his hair skewed, his eyes still sleepy. He thought it was funny that Steven wore an apron around his middle. Steven looked so lively and pleased when he was cooking. Mason couldn't help but wonder how lonely his life must have been before, living alone with no one to cook for.

"Hey, you're the first one up,'" Steven said. "It's all right. We'll get along just fine, just us."

Mason shrugged, sat down at the counter. He was surprised at how hungry he felt. Steven drowned a pancake in butter and syrup, and slid the plate to Mason with the need to please so plain and dire in his face. Mason wanted to reach out and scrub it clean.

"It looks great," he said, trying to sound enthusiastic as he dug in.

Out the kitchen window, Mason caught flashes of movement. He looked closer and recognized the boy next door wrestling a golden retriever over something in the grass.

"That's Jackson," Steven said. "About your age, I think. Kid loves baseball. You play baseball, Mason?"

Mason shook his head, the syrup sticky and sweet on his lips. He licked them.

Michael appeared in the doorway and said, "Mason's not an athlete."

"Mason's an artist," his mother said, trailing close behind. "Beautiful pictures, right baby?"

"I'm not an artist," Mason said, and shoveled more food in his mouth so he wouldn't have to talk about his pictures.

"Don't be modest," his mother said. "Boys don't get anywhere if they're modest."

"You got enough food there, Mace? That boy's gonna get fat eatin' with you," Michael said. Setting his own plate on the counter, he rubbed a hand over Steven's belly and said, "When are you due there, Stevie? Is it a boy or a girl?"

Steven swatted at him, went back to flipping pancakes.

Mason watched his mother fix her coffee—black, three sugars—and caught her stifling a laugh.

"Can I be excused?" he said.

His mother scanned his plate, which he had cleared so quickly his stomach hurt.

"Maybe if you show some manners," she said.

Mason thanked Steven for the pancakes and slid out the back door before anyone could stop him.

In the cool wet grass, Mason laid down and squinted in the sun. Clouds drifted slowly up above, and Mason picked out shapes. A train. A whale. A Pokémon. A dizzy, calm feeling spread over him, and then a shadow.

"You're new here, right?"

When Jackson spoke, Mason listened. There was something gritty in his voice, something old about it, he thought. Mason sat up on his elbows.

"My mother and I got here yesterday," he said.

"Right. Anyway, you play ball?"

Jackson spoke like he was running low on time. Mason shook his head.

"Well, you wanna learn?"

Mason wasn't sure. He had never been good at sports, a constant embarrassment back home in Pittsburgh where most boys idolized the Penguins or the Steelers or both. Mason wasn't cut out for that stuff. He looked back at the house now. Through the window, he could see Michael teasing his mother with strips of bacon. Offering them up, then eating them himself. She laughed. He kissed her cheeks.

"Sure," Mason said. "I'll play."

He thought Jackson looked pleased, but Jackson had a subtle face. A slightly removed expression. Mason took his spare mitt and fit it to his hand. It smelled like the woods smell after heavy rain, musty and sweet. Mason wondered if the smell would linger on his fingers after.

"You never played before?" Jackson said.

Mason said he'd played catch and all that in gym class, but he was never any good.

The boys took their places in the yard, standing about five yards apart. Jackson told Mason to "just catch it" when the ball came. Simple enough.

Raising his arms, Jackson pulled the ball around in a loose, fluid circle, letting it go with a practiced flick of his thin wrist. Mason had seen men move that way on television, and thought it was kind of beautiful. He got distracted by the movement, caught up in it, and the ball didn't arch as he expected it to; it darted, and Mason dropped hard to the ground when it smacked against his face.

"Oh, shit," Jackson said.

Crumpled on the ground, Mason clutched his eye. It throbbed and burned. His nose felt like it was running, but he checked it with his fingers. No blood. Jackson jogged over and crouched down next to him.

"Let me see it. Go on, move your hands," he said

Gently, Jackson peeled his fingers away from his face.

"Oh, Jesus," he said.

"What's it look like?" Mason asked, and was grateful when Jackson ignored it when his voice cracked.

"I wouldn't run out and get your picture taken," Jackson said. "But it really ain't so bad."

Mason bit his lip to keep himself from crying. Jackson plopped down in the grass and took his mitt off.

"You weren't kidding, huh? You're not very good at this," he said, and laughed.

Mason laughed a little, too. He couldn't tell if this boy was making fun of him or not.

"Jackson Pride," he said and offered his hand.

The boys shook, then slid back into silence. The day was heating up already. Mason didn't feel like crying anymore, but his face hurt and his cheek had gone a little numb. Jackson pushed his legs out straight and crossed them. His fingers pulled at the grass.

"I am sorry about that eye," he said.

Mason waved it off. He took his own mitt off and tossed it.

"Welcome to the neighborhood, huh?" Jackson said. "Where you from anyway?"

"Pittsburgh," Mason said.

"Why'd you move down here?"

Mason shrugged. He'd started pulling at the grass, too, and he could smell it now, rubbed the green into his fingers. Sweet and fragrant.

"Is your mom dating Steven?" Jackson asked.

"Steven's cousin," Mason said. "This is only temporary. Until we find our own place, you know."

"Where's your pop?" Jackson asked.

Mason shook his head. Jackson hummed.

"Yeah, I don't got one either anymore. Car accident when I was seven. Pretty ugly."

"I'm sorry," Mason said.

"You didn't kill him."

Mason felt stupid for saying he was sorry.

"Hey, look here," Jackson said.

Mason turned, and Jackson inspected him. Jackson's eyes squinted a little, and Mason didn't know if he was squinting in the sun or if he was just looking at him that hard.

"Yeah," he said. "Think you'll have a black eye there."

Jackson reached his fingers out and touched Mason's cheek, and Mason flinched, which made Jackson laugh for some reason.

"Boy, you're skittish," Jackson said, smiling and sun kissed.

Mason went back to tugging at the grass, and they sat that way for a while, until Michael called him back inside.

The skin around Mason's eye deepened to black, then aged into a lighter purple and stayed that way for days. Over the course of their first week in Virginia, he often inspected the bruise closely in the bathroom mirror, locking the door behind him. He would press his fingers into it, gingerly at first, then with a little more weight. He almost enjoyed the dull ache that sunk into his cheek. The prickling feeling that spread across his nose. Like he could knead the pain away.

In bed each night, he stayed up drawing in the light from the window above his bed. A porch light just outside. Mason had always liked to draw. He found it calming, engrossing. He was good at it, and he could forget about himself for a little while.

Mason drew new landscapes with soft grasses and the pastel gradient of light at dusk. He drew the old house in Pittsburgh. The yellow tile in the kitchen. The forest green front door. His mother had let him pick the color years ago. He drew Anna, softening her wispy curls by rubbing his thumb in circles against the paper.

He had not seen Jackson since that first day, but still he found the boy's face intriguing. There was something wrapped up in it, indecipherable like a knot of rope. He drew the sharp-cutting green in his eyes, and the buzz cut, his sandy-colored hair. He drew the bust of him, working down through his collar bones and shoulders. Mason was stuck on his lips. Like the Mona Lisa, he thought. Mason couldn't quite figure Jackson's expression.

In the end, he drew him smiling. A crooked smile like the one he wore when he had called Mason skittish. Mason had only ever heard that term in reference to animals, weak ones, prey.

Two weeks passed, and the black eye faded to yellow. Steven and Michael had started leaving early in the morning for the shop, and by the time Mason woke each day they were gone already. His mother wasn't working yet, and spent her time combing newspapers with Anna bouncing in her lap, and making phone calls, and reading pulp fiction by the blast of the window AC unit in the living room. Mason avoided her company; she avoided him back.

In the yard, one afternoon so hot the AC did almost nothing but make noise, Mason saw him again. Jackson came out with the mitts and dropped one of them in Mason's lap.

"Let's try this again," Jackson said. He had placed the ball inside the mitt he gave to Mason. "You start this time."

Jackson looked a little different than he had that first day, rounder somehow, more solid, or maybe Mason was just noticing more parts of him, treating him as a subject now that he had drawn him once already.

The first throw fell short, but Jackson sprang into action, snatching the ball up and throwing it back with surprising speed. Mason caught it only by the accuracy of the throw, as it wedged into the worn leather of the glove. A satisfying smack. The force of it prickling Mason's palm with pins and needles.

Mason's second throw was harder but less accurate, and Jackson still had to scoop the ball up from the ground. Still, Mason felt like he was getting the hang of it. He wasn't good yet, but maybe with some practice.

They went on like this for what felt like an hour, until the clouds swept over and a heavy rain blew in. The boys ran back inside, their T-shirts wetted through to bone. Mason's hair had gotten shaggy since the move, and Jackson scrubbed his hand through it.

"You're like a wet dog," he said.

Mason pawed his hand away and led Jackson through the kitchen and back into the bedroom. His mother had gone out for groceries with Anna, and as far as Mason knew Michael was still at the shop with Steven. They were alone.

Mason plopped down on the bed. The rain pounded on the roof.

"Nice place," Jackson said.

"No, it isn't," Mason said. "Don't be smart."

"No," Jackson said. "Scout's honor."

Jackson looked up at the rigged sheet.

"Not typical, is it?" he said, smiling like he had a secret.

Mason gave in and laughed a little.

"Suppose not," he said, dragging a towel through his hair.

Jackson made fast work of looking through his things. Mason was surprised, and a little touched, by how nosy he was. Kids back home were never curious about him. Mason's T-shirts were still balled up in the corner on the floor with mismatched pairs of socks folded into each other. His colored pencils were next to the bed, spilling out of their case. Mason leaned back and watched Jackson paw through all of his possessions.

"You draw," he said. Jackson picked up the green pencil Mason had used to color in his eyes just days—a new drawing, more accurate, he hoped—and before Mason could stop him, Jackson picked up the folder he kept his papers in and opened it.

"Is this me?" Jackson asked, a crease in between his eyes, just above his nose.

"That's just a sketch," Mason muttered.

The rain had picked up and the noise of it overwhelmed the sound inside the room so Jackson sounded far away, even though he was actually quite close. Jackson sat down on the bed next to Mason and scooted back so he could lean against the window. Mason thought he looked like a picture backlit like that, his face in shadow. A silver rim of light at the back of his neck. A picture you'd feel compelled to take.

"I think it's more than a sketch," Jackson said, turning his head for a better look at the drawing.

And Mason knew he was right. The amount of detail in the drawing was embarrassing. The shading across the face and the careful depiction of his hair. The touch of collarbone peeking out from his crewneck T-shirt. Mason didn't like to flatter himself, but he considered it one of his best.

"I'd say you're better at drawing than I am at baseball," Jackson said.

The bedroom door was slightly ajar, not fully open, not fully closed.

"You got others?" Jackson asked.

Mason nodded, gestured at the folder in his hands. Jackson set his own drawing aside and leafed through the rest of them.

"You're really good," he said.

Mason thought he sounded genuinely impressed.

"You wanna teach me how to draw sometime?"

"You wanna learn?" Mason asked, dumbfounded.

Jackson spit in his palm and offered it to Mason. Reluctantly, Mason shook it. Their grasp was wet and disgusting.

"You're supposed to spit, too," Jackson said, and laughed, taking his hand back. "I'll see you tomorrow, Mace."

He left the house on his own, as if he lived there, too.

The summer carried on. The boys played baseball in the mornings before the sun beat down in full. After, they retreated to the shade of the house, where Mason showed Jackson the intricacies of line work and shading. Jackson was a slow learner, but he admired art in a way Mason had never thought to admire it before. It was just something he did.

Jackson's favorite thing to flip through was a series of animals Mason had started a few of weeks into their lessons. Mason liked the reptiles best. Lizards and bearded dragons and turtles. But the most impressive drawings were the birds, ranging from large intricate peacocks, to small, rust-chested robins. Several times Mason caught Jackson smoothing over the birds with the palm of his hand, as if he thought he could feel their feathers. As if he could pet them.

"They have a great sense of direction, birds. They always know where they are and in relation to what. And their bones are hollow, not dense like ours," Jackson said.

It was raining again that day, and they had skipped baseball altogether. Mason stopped drawing and watched Jackson instead.

"That's how they can just pick up and go. They can fly anywhere."

The boys were crouched on Mason's mattress again, the rain pattering the window. Mason had learned to read Jackson, the tilt of his lips when he was thinking. The curve of his chin and the shadow it cast on his thin neck. The soft lump of his Adam's apple.

Mason's body leaned into him all by itself. And Jackson smelled like cut grass and dryer sheets and mud and the eucalyptus chips he kept in his pockets and sucked on sometimes, in the mornings like chewing tobacco. His lips hovered close to Jackson's neck, which had very small, peach-like hairs on it. Mason thought he could touch his lips down on that skin, only for a moment.

Jackson stood up and put the drawings down on the bed.

"I should get home," he said. "My mom's gonna need help with the dinner tonight. Fried chicken."

Mason nodded. The long-forgotten drawing still in his lap, and the cerulean pencil in his hand.

"So, I'll see you tomorrow," Jackson said.

Mason nodded again and said, "Right, yeah."

When Jackson left, Mason could see out into the hallway, the bedroom door wide open now. Michael was standing out there, surely close enough to hear them. He seemed taller, Mason thought. A trick of the light, maybe, the long stretch of hallway making him look bigger, too. And now it was only him and Mason.

Michael's workpants were spread with dark lines of grease and motor oil. His steel-toed boots, size twelve, worn leather. They must have thudded down the hallway, but Mason had not heard them.

"What's goin' on?" Michael asked.

Mason took the drawing of the birds and slid it back into the folder with the others.

"Nothing," he said.

In August, Mason's mother got a job at the only diner they could walk to. Mason and Jackson started visiting in the afternoons for free shakes and fries. The place was straight out of the 1950's, shiny metal wrapping the exterior. Inside, the boys would sit at the counter with Anna's stroller nestled in between their swivel stools.

The women at the diner enjoyed their company. So damn cute just sitting there, sharing shakes. Jackson always let Mason have the maraschino cherry on top of their chocolate milkshakes. Mason's mother was more reserved, but she smiled at Jackson the same way she smiled at Mason when she thought he couldn't see her. Doe-eyed, reverent.

Mason had tried to forget all about that rainy afternoon, and Jackson never brought it up. They just kept going along together, and everything was fine.

On the way home from the diner one afternoon, the boys walked on opposite sides of the road kicking loose stones back and forth. It was the dead of August, smack in the middle of a heatwave. They baked in the sun and sought out every inch of shade. Mason pushed Anna's stroller and made sure her legs were covered by the hood of it.

"I'm bakin' in this sun, Mace," he called, rubbing sweat from his face with his grass-stained T-shirt. "How's that baby?"

Mason stood a little straighter, looked down at Anna sleeping with flushed cheeks.

"Almost home," he said, more to himself than to Jackson.

In the front yard, Michael and Steven sat with a cooler of cheap beers between them. Their thick canvas work pants slouched around their waists. Mason thought it was odd that they were home in the middle of the day and parked Anna's stroller in the shade.

"Mason Grey," Michael called.

His voice held none of the sweetness of the women at the diner. Mason hated when he used his first and middle names, like he was some big man, like he was a father.

"Get over here," he said. "What are you walkin' around all day for?"

Mason told him they had only been at the diner to visit his mother. Steven started in on another beer.

"Well, why you ain't tell anybody?" Michael said.

Mason rolled his eyes, turned back to Jackson, who hovered close to Anna's stroller.

"Don't you look at him," Michael said. "You look at me. Why didn't you tell anybody?"

Mason turned back and shrugged, exhausted. He was so hot his whole back had sweated through his T-shirt, the fabric clinging to his skin.

"You keepin' secrets?" Michael asked.

"No," Mason said.

"Don't take that tone. How old are you?" he asked. "Thirteen?"

Michael pulled a cigarette from his pocket and lit it. It made Mason's throat burn even more, just to think of smoking when it was over a hundred degrees outside.

Mason nodded. Thirteen. His birthday had passed in July. He couldn't tell where Michael was going with all this, but his shoulders were getting tense the longer Michael kept them in the yard, and the sweat seemed to cool too quickly on his body now. A chill ran up his spine and his arms broke out in goosebumps.

"I found your pictures," Michael said. "Found your drawings of that boy over there."

"So?" Mason said, but he felt the blood drain from his face.

"So, I've seen it," Michael said. "You and that faggot neighbor every afternoon, doing God knows what."

Michael tapped dead ash from the end of his cigarette and it smoldered in the grass.

Of course, Mason had heard the word before, but never with such certainty. The boys at school were just boys. Young, and stupid, flimsy in the ways they flung out insults. On their lips, the word faggot could just as easily be the word loser, or idiot, or pansy, or fuckhead, or jerk. Michael gave new weight to it. Next to him, Steven didn't even flinch.

"You like birds," Michael asked.

Mason looked at him, confused. He wanted even just a sip of water.

"I saw you been drawin' some fancy birds."

Mason swallowed and said sure, he liked birds.

"I know he likes birds," Michael said, nodding at Jackson.

Michael stretched an arm back underneath his chair, where a small cardboard box rested. Mason hadn't noticed it before. Just two men in their folding chairs, and a cooler of beers on a hot day. Mason hadn't noticed the box, and watched as Michael worked his hand inside of it, and in a split moment, he pulled out a barn swallow. Mason recognized it from the nature books they had been using all summer long, to draw from.

"You like this kinda bird?" Michael said.

Its chest was a creamy white, its wings so blue it nearly camouflaged against the sky. There was a kerchief of burnt red-orange around the bird's neck, and the color extended over its face. Mason watched as Michael dangled the bird by one spindly leg, and its wings flapped, and its body twisted.

"Where'd you get that?" Mason asked. His throat was like sandpaper.

The bird struggled, and with a clean, almost tinny crack, its leg snapped. Mason jumped and took a step back. It was the only time Michael looked nervous. Mason caught that look in his eyes. Just a flicker of concern.

Gently, Michael put the bird down in the grass between where he and Mason stood. The animal writhed and made only a little noise. Mason could hear Jackson breathing close behind him.

"You know, my daddy let us have a rabbit when we were kids," Michael said. "He was white all over with just a single spot on his back between the shoulders."

Michael stood up a little straighter, and Mason heard his back crack several times like the fire-cracker pop of every knuckle on a single hand.

"Did you know rabbits can kick so hard they break their own backs when they're scared enough and trapped enough?"

Mason did not know that.

"Well, they can," Michael said. "That rabbit got himself stuck in the baby gate my mother kept in the kitchen, and when I got home from school he was just layin' there all still and a little crooked. My daddy had me shoot him in the backyard. Put him out of his misery."

Steven sat still as a statue now. His drink paused to hover at his sternum, halfway to his mouth. He looked as shocked as Mason imagined his own face, no longer bruised, just a little sunburnt from the walk. Mason turned and fixated on the cooler, the ice melting down to nothing. He wanted to splash that melty water all over his skin. He wanted to drink it.

"Kill it," Michael said.

Mason looked back at him and felt his mouth fall open.

Michael nudged the bird forward with his foot. The animal was hardly moving anymore.

"Go on and do it," Michael said.

But Mason couldn't move. He looked down at the bird and its eye was just a small, black bead of ink. Mason's mind stretched back to the diner and the milkshake, and the salt on the fries, and the sugared cherry on his tongue. Something wet and delicious. He looked back down at the bird and knew he couldn't do it.

Michael pulled a paper from his pocket and unfolded it. It was the drawing of Jackson. His green eyes. The yellow Mason had placed so carefully over his head. It had been difficult, Mason remembered, to get it right, the shallow buzz cut almost imperceptible to the eye.

Michael offered up the drawing, and Mason took it and folded it along the creases and put it in his pocket.

"Put that thing out of its misery," Michael said.

He walked off into the dark cavity of the house, and Mason watched him go.

Mason does not think of the bird every day. He does not have visions of the body on the ground. He does not hear its squawks, its little noises, and he is not haunted by the beauty of its feathers. Rarely does he imagine the feeling of the bird's soft tufts beneath his fingertips.

When Mason looks at other birds, he does not flinch at them. He does not see them as reverberations of the past, and he does not think of that afternoon with the sun beating down his back, and, when pressed, he cannot even remember exactly what Jackson's face had looked like.

It was a young and lonely summer. It was a long time ago now.

He snapped its neck with the flat of his thumb, pushed hard into the ground.

EVERYTHING IN GOOD TIME

I had never been in a house without a TV in it. The quiet announced itself as we walked through the front door and it was like the feeling of forgetting something. I checked my pockets. Car keys, cell phone. An aluminum wrapper clinging to a chewed-up piece of gum. Everything was where it should have been. Martin led us down the long, narrow hallway, through the galley kitchen and, at last, into the wood-paneled living room. He took our jackets, and we shifted our feet on the carpeting, waiting for him to return.

The room was on the smaller side for the amount of money Martin had spent on the house, but on the larger side for our standards. The front wall was entirely made of windows and outside of them we could see the weeping branches of an evergreen mid-winter, weighted with snow. The carpeting was shag, burnt orange, and cleaner than I'd ever imagined shag carpeting could get, even new. And the walls were dark wood slats running vertically towards the ceiling.

"Drinks," Martin said, popping back in.

It wasn't a question.

Lo said, "I'll take a glass of wine."

I asked for a beer, but I knew Martin wouldn't have any. He wasn't that kind of drinker. Martin was eager to please. He gave the overall impression of a middle child, or maybe the youngest, always trying to measure up to something. He brought me bourbon.

"Thanks," I said, accepting the lowball glass. The ice cubes swirled around each other like magnets not quite touching.

Lo sipped her glass of wine. She was looking very elegant and stuffy. She had on that cream, cable knit turtleneck sweater that always made her look like someone's wife on TV. Her lipstick was the same shade as her cabernet. Her nails were painted over with a clear film of shine. I sipped my bourbon. It burned my throat.

"So, what do you think of it," Martin asked.

He looked a little desperate, alone in front of us. I felt sorry for him. He'd bought the house while Lo and I were away on our annual pilgrimage to Vermont, where we had first met six years ago. By that point Karen had left him, and he had closed on a house outside of the city, and would we want to come over and see it? Would we have the time to catch up soon? And how were we doing? What was new? What had we been up to lately? On a whim, we agreed.

I surveyed the living room more closely. There were folded-up boxes in the far corner. There was a bloated garbage bag behind the sleek love-seat Martin had most likely bought full price. There was a fireplace in the center of the longest wall. Unlit; shallow mantel. The walls were blank and faceless and gave an overall hollow impression like a college dorm room cast in harsh fluorescents.

"It's wonderful," Lo said. "Isn't it?" She turned to me and nudged my arm, so I agreed.

It was the first time I'd seen her face full-on all evening. We had both gotten dressed in a hurry, having rushed through weekend errands, scarfed-down lunches, the weekly cleaning of the apartment. And on the drive over, it had been snowing. Big flakes, fast flakes. I had focused only on the road, though I had imagined what her face looked like beside me. Eyes: squinted, then bored. Lips: moderately pursed (this weather!). Cheeks: flushed, always. And now, her face turned to me, looked at me. I wanted, suddenly, to be alone with her.

"It's really something," I said, nodding approval and glancing around the room again.

The ceiling was too high for comfort. You could almost forget about it. And, with the windows and the tree just outside, and the wooden walls, and the grassy texture of the carpeting—it felt like we were outside in the woods. I didn't know what else to say. "Love those windows. Must get great natural light."

"Great natural lighting," Lo repeated and I hummed.

I resisted asking about Karen. Gone three months before he closed on the house. This lonely place was to be Martin's lifeboat in the rocky ocean of divorce, or perhaps, the basis for their recoupling. But Lo and I doubted that. Late at night, we often wondered at how they had unraveled. And how they had unraveled so quickly.

"Slowly making progress," Martin said, shrugging. "Hoping for hardwood under this carpeting," he said, tapping his feet on the puffed flooring.

Martin half-sat, half-leaned on the arm of the armchair next to the sofa Lo and I had sunken into. His broad shoulders slumped forward a little in his thick flannel shirt. His beard had grown since we had seen him last. He looked a little like Paul Bunyan. Or Charles Manson. Divorce, I reasoned, could make sane people crazy. Ever so slightly, Lo's shoulders stiffened against me on the couch.

"Well." Martin gulped his drink—something clear, more liquid than water—and carefully appraised his living room one more time. "I certainly think it has potential, anyway."

Lo hummed her agreement. And we all came to another sputtering stop, sitting there, not speaking, not knowing what to say.

"It's very quiet," I offered.

"In a good way," Lo finished on my behalf.

I swirled the ice cubes in my drink more firmly so they clinked against each other. It was the only noise in the room.

Dinner was a rack of lamb and mint-something. It wasn't quite a sauce, more so like a salsa. It tasted good, though the lamb was overcooked and dry. Martin was at least trying to play host. Before the split, we had had these dinners once or twice a month, the four of us alternating apartments. Mine and Lo's: squat ceilings, tiny kitchen, the smell of dinner filling up the bedroom and the house, plates rested in laps and wine glasses kissing stains on the coffee table. Martin and Karen's: horizontal, three rooms, each of them the same size and width and connected by a single hallway, a drop-leaf dining table, board games everywhere.

Lo started in on her third glass of wine, and Martin refilled my bourbon. I had the prickling feeling he had been drinking long before we had pulled up in his driveway. The smell of him, the clumsy movement of his arms and hands. Our plates looked barbaric at this stage, nothing but stripped bones and minty residue. Martin swallowed more of his own drink, which seemed to refill as if by magic.

"How's work been," Lo asked, admirably pumping up the conversation.

"Oh, it's so-so, really," Martin said, his cheeks pink as shrimps.

Lo nodded. Her foot grazed mine beneath the table.

"Have you—have you heard any news from Karen lately?" I asked.

Beside me, Lo stretched like she was struggling against her own skin. I knew the look she wanted to give me. Daggers. But she righted herself and took another bite of lamb.

Martin adjusted himself and said, "I forgot. I have a loaf of bread heating up in the oven."

He excused himself, shedding the cloth napkin from his lap onto the table. Lo turned her head very slowly to look at me. In her eyes: dark, glitter, the blade of a knife. I forked through the remainder of the meal left on my plate. Martin returned, a loaf of steaming bread in his mitted hands. All three of us ate from it in silence. I mopped the mint salsa from my plate with it and thought about marriage.

I first met Lois when I was twenty-one. I had been distrustful of the word lesbian. It was a little like the word vagina. It sounded like something floral and repulsive, like a fungus, and nobody liked it. Still, I resisted my repulsion. Lo helped.

We lived in Montpelier, then. There wasn't much to do there but read and work and lounge around the house together. I was living on a farm my uncle had let me use out of kindness. Lois was living at home with her mother who was dying (breast cancer). In the winter, we proctored ski school. In the summer, I worked at the local bookstore and Lois worked at the bakery across the street. She used to bring me loaves of freshly baked bread. Ours was an old-timey kind of love. A small-town affair, and homemade bread, and holding hands to keep them warm all winter. I was there when her mother died. I held her when she wailed. I had never seen a dead person before. I had never heard a woman make such painful, unadulterated, animal noises before.

What we had been through—it was hard to say exactly. It felt like too many things at once, and all of it had tethered us. We were coupled. I would always be the one who had been there when her mother died. She would always be the woman I had finally allowed myself to love; strong and tired, heartbroken and joyful, bursting. Floured pants and the smell of golden crust. Flushed cheeks, the gap between her two front teeth. Her humor. I once found a lump of dough in her hair post-sex.

To this day, and for these reasons, I cannot imagine leaving her.

***

After dinner, we played Uno, which I hated. Lo looked mischievous and beautiful behind her spread of cards. Her eyes exposed above them betrayed the smile she must have worn on her lips. Martin was unbearable. He kept his cards upside-down on the table and had to sort through them every time his turn came up, again and again. It was exhausting. For once, I kept my mouth shut, and Lo placed a gauntlet of cards, all of them changing the color or adding three to my pile, or skipping my turn.

At last, she said, "Uno," so smug.

I couldn't tell if I wanted to kiss her or quit and go home and sleep. The house was still so quiet. The branches of the evergreen tapped lightly on the wall of windows, a brittle raking sound that gave me goosebumps. The bourbon had made me restless. Across from me, Martin sighed. He had refilled his drink again. His eyes kept moving to the doorway of the galley kitchen, planting all his expectation that empty space.

"Your turn, Marty," I said, prodding him.

He sorted his cards, then placed three green cards face-up on the pile. "Uno," he said.

Lo groaned and plucked cards from the deck until she got the right color. I still had half the deck in my hands. How was Martin beating me? I put down two green cards and Lo changed the color. We kept going. We were silent and mindless for a while. I kept track of Martin with small glances. I wanted to tell him we missed Karen, too, but I didn't know if that would make him feel better or worse. I remembered Lo's mantra of choice: *Everything in good time.* I tried to honor this, her words.

External life is linear. You can't rush it. You can't push it forward. And there is no way of going back. You just have to sit still in the middle part— and there is so much of the middle part—and play your cards.

We met Karen when we left Montpelier. Lo's mother had been dead two years and we had sold her house and made arrangements to store the bigger pieces of the furniture—the things Lo couldn't stand to part with—in the basement of my uncle's farmhouse. We hid these pieces under draped white sheets like rich people do in the movies. I remember feeling like we had just bought a haunted place as I looked out on the spread of ghosted couches and armoires. We were the unsuspecting newlyweds moving into the old, haunted house on the hill.

For two years, we lived in my uncle's farmhouse. Sometimes, we heard creaks in the night, though Lo assured me I was only dreaming. *You watch too much television*, she'd say, stroking my hair, clutching me to her chest until I slept again. There is no comfort greater than Lo's soft body, warm and fit to mine. Physical and unmarred by language, by voice. Sometimes I think our bodies are drawn to one another. It's not so much about the soul, but what it's like to hear their heart beating in the middle of the night, to feel their leg draped casually over your own.

For some time, we imagined the farmhouse and the land surrounding as our saviors. Having studied the environment, Lo would know how to treat the land well, and I knew everyone in town from the bookstore, had seen the workings of small business, tourist seasons. Late at night, in bed, we joked about lesbian farmers. We could get goats; we could make cheese.

But the house was drafty and old. The floorboards were creaky and unfinished. The oven may have been leaking gas, slowly killing us. Lo had applied to a job in Boston, a non-profit that focused on the cleanliness of oceans. When she got the job, I applied for a position at a charter school teaching English to eighth graders. We boarded up the house for winter and left.

In Boston, Lo met Karen in a coffee shop. It felt like a small-town fortune, to meet someone, casually, in a coffee shop. To befriend them. It comforted us. Karen was immediately a welcome thing. She had long brown hair and plump hips she wore candidly and comfortably. She read voraciously and she and I had started swapping books. She liked to do those silly pottery classes, where you can paint your own mugs and plates. Together, she and Lo made a full dining set at the one pottery place in Brookline that served wine.

We treated her, at first, as a couple might a puppy or a baby. A galvanizing presence, something new and strange to interact with. Karen somehow felt so necessary—it was sometimes difficult to have coupled so young, so early in our twenties with no room to grow separately, or move apart, or stretch outside the bubble of the two of us. As much as we loved the bubble, we were quietly intrigued by our intruder.

When Karen met Martin, we were admittedly disappointed she was straight.

I didn't believe in Uno anymore. Adults should not play games like this. Lo won (of course) and Martin (we knew) was shielding tears of disappointment, failure. There were only three cards left limply in his hand.

The dinner was too much for him. Alone, he was just Martin. Alone in the house, he could arrange each room and unpack boxes. He could pick out pieces of furniture—loveseat, armchair, coffee table. But with the two of us there in front of him, it was all the more apparent who was missing. Lo and I were like a walking reminder of his loneliness. We were a couple, and he was just a man in an empty house, stripped of his better half. He had no better half. Lo and I sat together on his couch, drinking his drinks, beating him at his own game.

Lo's face had turned so suddenly to mine when she won, that well-known spark of connection, just as jolting as it always had been. Our eye contact, a regular flirtation. We had grown up together; we had grown together. We had come to fill our days with countless errands, and bills paid, and dishes washed and left to dry face-down on the countertop. We spent so much time in the logistical swirl of living, a kind of bliss. We still had our moments. Her face confronted all of my senses. My head gone numb. My mind swam at the sight of her, her eyes cut over the flush of Uno cards. Her bold movements, the remnants of the bread ripped from the center of the table, and the pressure of her fingers on my leg. The feeling of her fingers; Martin had lost this. I wondered: had he ever even had it?

"Good game," I said, when the Uno deck had been tucked into its flimsy cardboard casing.

Lo smiled. "You're pissed you didn't win," she said.

The wine was getting to her. She was relaxing into herself again. I was so relieved she hadn't used the words "wonderful" or "charming," something vaguely housewife-approving. Even her turtleneck sweater seemed calmer now, less Hallmark.

"I'm not *that* mad about it," I said.

"Remember when you flipped the chess board?" Lo asked.

I had (only once) flipped the chess board after losing.

"I do," I said, feigning reluctance.

"Remember when you yelled at Martin when he bankrupted you in Monopoly?" Lo was beaming. It rubbed off on all of us and soon Martin was smiling, too. I was amazed by her ability to do that, to change the air in the room like you might spread fresh sheets across a mattress.

"I remember that," Martin said, shaking his head. "You called me a 'fucker,' I think."

"So, I'm competitive," I said, hands raised in innocence. "Sue me!" My drink was empty. I rattled the ice. "You really don't have any beer in this house?"

"Feels too pathetic," Martin said, in good enough humor. His words came out a little slurred, their edges rounded. "I'm a bachelor now, living alone," he said, and Lo made a sympathetic face, her brow marked with lines of tension.

"It's not that sad," she said and placed her hand very lightly on his thigh.

But Martin's face had changed, had drained itself of life.

"What?" Lo asked.

"You said *that* sad." He shook his head, swallowed his drink and coughed a little.

We all got quiet again, the room unbearably stiff.

It seemed, to me, that there was nothing else to say, so I said, "I think we should talk about Karen."

It happened not unlike you might imagine. Things were smooth for a while. It was like driving on autopilot. We were couples and friends. We were a unit of four. Martin and I played our roles well (the "men"). We talked about sports. I feigned my way through many conversations, as did he—we would soon learn that neither of us like sports. Lo and Karen shared recipes at holidays, enjoyed cooking together and working through bottles of wine; they liked going to the movies and kept a pulse on what was new. Martin and I followed them around like dogs. It was all very normative.

The dinners gave rhythm to our lives. We were comfortable as family, and yet we still used our socializing voices, still dressed a little better when we saw each other, still gossiped relentlessly afterwards. (*Did you catch Martin's hand sliding into the ass pocket of her jeans?*) We settled into our lives. Montpelier—the farm house, the ghosted furniture, the loaves of bread and discount books—all felt very far away, as if from someone else's life. Lo missed her mother. We still used her sterling silverware on special occasions.

Looking back, it all seems very ordinary, satisfying in its own way. Looking closely, there were signs.

Karen would (sometimes) run her fingers along the flank of Lo's thin forearm when they passed by each other in the kitchen. Karen would (sometimes) rest her hand just above my knee when we were sitting on the couch, playing games. Karen would (sometimes) admit a kind of fascination she had with certain women. *They're just so stunning!* Lo and I had taken these instances passively as we most commonly saw them: the straight woman's curiosity at the manifested lesbian. Karen was not the worst we had seen; she was, we admitted, kind of funny about it. *How do you guys—do it, though?*

That night, it had been Karen and Martin's turn to host. Lo made a loaf of sourdough; I bought a bottle of wine. Karen made Shakshouka and displayed a medley of olives in tiny glass bowls, all of them painted with intricate designs. We heated the bread in the oven before serving.

Martin was happy to see us. The two of us talked while setting the table. Lo stayed behind in the kitchen, sipping wine already and telling Karen all about the nature of abandoned dolphins in the Boston Harbor.

We ate. The Shakshouka was ripe on our tongues, the fatty olives juiced in our mouths, tart and fragrant. The bread was used to sop the sauce and clean our plates and fill our stomachs. We all raved about the food. Martin looked very proud of Karen. They had been married a year before, and it was as if his body couldn't contain itself under so much excitement and joy. His cheeks were constantly red, as if they'd been dipped in something sweet and permanent. He was, we could tell, even a little embarrassed by how much he loved his wife, how evident it was on him, how openly he wore his love and how he simply couldn't help it. He had to show it.

"Okay," Karen said. The plates had been cleared (by Martin) and the wine was from the third bottle that evening. "I have a kind of proposal. Proposition?" She steadied herself. She stood in front of us. She seemed nervous, but buoyed by her own nervousness somehow. And then slowly, tentatively, confidently, she pulled the sweater off first.

The sweater. A pilling woolly crewneck she had once told us had been a gift from her ex-boyfriend's mother, carted over all the way from Ireland. We thought she must have been warm from all the wine, the food, good company and laughter. Underneath the sweater she wore a cotton long-sleeved T-shirt. Her fingers toyed around the bottom edges of the fabric, then slipped underneath and slowly pulled the T-shirt up and over her head. We were silent.

The room felt dead and still as the walls comprising it, flat and smooth and cool to the touch, the pimpled coat of paint. We watched her. We felt like voyeurs, dirty and breathless. As Karen stepped out of her faded blue jeans, Lo's hand rested on my leg and I questioned what it meant there. Martin's eyes held a new kind of tension, his lips just slightly parted.

Karen stood in front of us. Behind her, the television seemed to frame her from where it rested, anchored to the wall. Her breasts, bared now from her thin lace bra, were like two cantaloupes. Or rather, one canta-loupe, halved and placed there flat-side down. She was taller than I ever realized. Bigger, too. She filled the room. She bit her lip. She looked at us. She was still wearing her mid-calf socks, a pair I recognized with a shock as one of my own. And I remembered we had swapped, by accident, at the gym one evening.

Lo's hand was still warming the skin of my thigh. I stared at my socks on Karen's slender feet, then let my eyes trail upward. Her curved legs, her hips the shape of a heart, the skin like cream and smooth as butter. Her stomach softly muscled. Her arms long and thickly bicep-ed.

By the time I made it to her face, she was close to tears. She looked less invigorated by herself and, strangely, far more beautiful than she had before. Her eyes, water-swelled, bluish gray lagoons, pitted on either side of her long nose. Martin cleared his throat, and the sound made us un-comfortable. It took us seconds more to recover from the noise, and Lo's hand moved ever-so-slightly upward on my leg, then removed itself, only to touch back down again at the nape of my neck where it petted my skin very slowly, very softly. Did she want this? What was there to want?

"This is what I want," Karen said, her voice soft and foreign, as if filtered through a gramophone.

We waited for Martin. His shocked body flinched of the nerves all up and down his arms. The flicker of a finger. He sat with stiff posture, leaned slightly forward on the edge of the couch. His arms were bent, his long hands resting flat on his thighs. His lips were slightly parted. He was clean shaven then. His eyes wide, bright. He blinked and came back to life, as if a station had just come through clearer on the radio. Something was back inside of him again, alive and breathing, and, yes, moving. He stood and walked to her. His arms were limp and lifeless by his side, his head bowed like a boy both intrigued by and terrified of sex.

Lo petted the skin on my neck, that finger striking a careful rhythm. I would wait, I decided. I would wait for her to move. I would do nothing but watch Karen's eyes swim. Her skin bared. Her lips quivered, and she licked them. Nervously, so as to remove all salaciousness from the act of licking lips when naked. And still, Lo's finger touched down on my skin.

Martin was flustered as he dug our coats out from the closet. Lo had her arms folded over her chest, shoulders peaked as though she were cold. I had put my foot in my mouth, and now, I tried to bite my tongue. Martin could barely look at us.

"I just don't know if this was a good idea," he said.

"Come on, the lamb was good," Lo said. She nudged my arm.

"You made bread," I said, sounding simple.

"God, shut up!" Martin turned. His arms hung low like an ape's and our jackets in his hands pooled on the floor by his feet. I didn't like that my coat was touching the floor. Lo, likely sensing I might say so, stepped directly in front of me.

"Marty," she said. "We didn't mean to upset you. I think—we're all just trying to navigate this."

Martin breathed heavily.

"Honestly, I think it was a pretty successful evening," Lo said, which was clearly the wrong thing to say because Martin twitched. The movement was halfway between a shrug and the physical uproar at a referee's bad call.

"Do you know what this feels like?" he asked.

Lo took a deep breath and said, "No. I don't."

I could only see the back of her. Her hair was in a messy bun now and small wisps had been left behind at the softly curved nape of her neck.

"What does it feel like," she said, oozing compassion.

Martin took a more conscious breath, deep and labored. Lo retreated to stand beside me again, and our arms were nearly touching.

"Do you think she's a lesbian?" Martin asked. Our coats were still crumpled on the floor. He was losing himself. "She won't even talk to me now. And of course, I've fucking tried. I've tried everything. Do you think she's a fucking lesbian?"

Lo bit her lip, hard. "I don't know," she said, so Martin looked to me. I stalled, then said, "Maybe."

"I married a fucking dyke," Martin said, slapping his wide, flat palm against the wall.

We flinched, not so much at the sound of his skin slapping wood, more so at the word, which sounded tinny and hard coming out of his mouth. Like biting down on a bit of tin foil, or like a hammer to the head.

"No offense," he said, swiping hair from his forehead, revealing beads of sweat spread across the skin of his forehead. "What a fucking nightmare."

Lo stifled a snort, more shocked than amused.

"You think this is funny," Martin said, not missing a beat now.

"No," Lo said quickly. "We don't."

"Yes, you do," he said. He sounded so sure I almost believed him.

"You come in here all sympathetic and underneath all this bullshit, you think I'm hilarious, don't you? I'm just one of those pathetic men you hate."

There was a bubble of spit on his lip I couldn't take my eyes from. Lo, for the first time all evening, was speechless.

"It's not funny," I said, finding my voice. "It is a nightmare. And I'm sorry, we know that. Whether Karen's gay or not, there's something in her that she doesn't know how to get to. That's very sad, don't you think?" His brow furrowed, but he stayed quiet. "And we like you. We don't want you to be with a lesbian. That's not funny at all. It's just sad."

Consider Karen, I thought. Alone and lonely, desperate maybe. Had she been trapped? We had been pulled so close to her that night, the three of us in the living room. A joint movement of mismatched hands on her bared skin. The feeling of Lo's hand wrapped so tightly around the back of my neck. The wet warm of her skin tight up against my own, never moving, though our bodies had moved.

I had seen, my eyes half-sleepy, half-opened. Martin's lips pressed down into Karen's clavicle. And with that definitive loving touch, we had disbanded, untangled ourselves from this strange, amorphous mass we'd fallen into. The air turned slick and cool, no longer warm, liquid. But really, it had taken months to extricate ourselves completely. Karen stopped talking to us. Lo had made attempts at first, though halfheartedly. I stayed quiet. It felt so much easier to leave it all in the past. To allow the night to take up the space of shameful dreams, old childhood nightmares.

Standing in the vestibule with the dark woods all around us, Lo rested her head on my shoulder.

"You wanna come back in," Martin asked, sounding calmer than we had seen him.

Maybe, I thought, we had really made it through.

"That depends," Lo said. "Are you gonna take your clothes off?"

She smiled at her own joke. I laughed. I could feel us pulling safely to the other side of conflict. But Martin's face flickered and changed again. And there was, I could see, something genuinely mad about him. More Manson than Bunyan now.

"Always a joke with you," he said, as the last bit of softness left his expression.

Martin dropped our coats fully to the floor like a towel discarded after a hot shower. I didn't like it that his hands were empty now, exposed. I imagined them doing horrible things to us. I imagined them wrapped around Lo's swan neck. Long, thin, white as the pallid face of the moon. I imagined the pulse of her carotid blipping under the pressure of his fingers. I thought of the marks those fingers could make on her skin, then shook myself a little. What was it Lo always said? *You watch too much television.*

I noticed, for the first time, Martin was a foot or two taller than I was. And his arms, despite his tame line of work–an office job somewhere– were working arms, thick and rugged in an old flannel shirt. And we were alone with him in a house in the middle of the woods. And everything was so quiet, because we weren't simply alone in the house together. We were alone together, period. My mind stretched back to the drive up to this old house, and the thick snowfall on the iced back roads. It had taken us twenty minutes from the highway.

Standing there so close together, Lo's hand slipped easily into the pocket of my khaki pants. And I said, "I think we should go."

Martin still stood in front of the doorway. Slowly, I stooped and took our coats from where they rested. I handed Lo's over and she put it on, replacing her hand inside my pocket as soon as her arms had pushed through each of her sleeves. Suddenly, I felt very warm, so I folded my coat and let it rest in the crook of my elbow. And all was quiet again.

External life is linear. There is no pushing it forward, no way to move into the past. And so, we stood there in the middle, the place between what was to come and what we had put behind us. The three of us: two lesbians and a jolted husband, like a crude street joke. The foyer smelled of firewood and the cooler smell of falling snow. Inside my pocket: a subtle, nervous movement, as Lo's fingers worked their way around the car keys.

HOME FOR IT

The house smells like cedar and cinnamon from Mom's candles. I resist glancing the urn she insists on keeping in the kitchen. He loved to watch her cook, and he read cookbooks like they were novels: front-to-back. Mom cites these things as reasons, justification, for keeping his oblong pot of ashes right next to the oblong pot of granulated sugar. Earlier on, about two years ago now, when we were still slapstick with shock, we sometimes joked about what might happen if we ever mixed them up. A body cake, Mom said one afternoon, and we both laughed so hard we cried. We remembered it was actually him up there.

I drop my bag on the floor in the living room and flop onto the paisley sofa, the fabric cool and textured against my back through the thinner fabric of my T-shirt. I long for my cat Juno, the weight of her and the curl of her soft tail against my clavicle when she rests on top of my chest, sleeping. Last night, Haley made me homemade ravioli with garlic parmesan and the three of us—me, her, and the cat—watched a B-list monster movie to take my mind off things. I check my phone but it's dead from the eight-hour train ride home. Twenty-two years old, I still can't remember to bring a charger home with me.

Mom sinks into the couch across from mine. Privately, I wish she would lift my legs and sit by my feet the way she used to. I stretch out further, as if to stave off that fantasy.

"So," she says.

I take a big breath and hug a pillow to my chest. "So."

We watch Animal Planet, because Mom has committed to the life of a young widow and has taken to the dog shows. All her stories now are peppered with the lives of selfless caregivers at little-known shelters, the heartworms in a young lab puppy that led to his untimely death, the happy ending for a young family in Detroit who travelled all the way to Florida to adopt a greyhound when they closed the racing tracks last year. Tonight, we watch as a team of rescuers do their best to corner a stray pit bull they've found by the side of a major highway in Virginia.

I look over at my mother, but she is glued to the television. An orb of warm light spreads over her—the checkered lamp next to the couch— and for a moment there, she looks close to holy. I wonder what it will be like when she dies, too. The house will be so empty, arcane without my parents moving through it. Maybe Teddy will live here, I think. The oldest, the boy. Oldest boys are always inheriting things like houses and money.

I study my mother—salt-and-pepper hair; sharp nose; round eyes, underlined by dark circles I think make her look very pretty. Her right arm is folded over her stomach and her left elbow rests on the arm of the couch; her left hand just barely supports her head, her fingers spread over her cheek.

On the TV screen, day descends to night, and the rescuers work large flashlights through heavy brush. Their hiking boots crunch through dirt, stick, and gravel. I've lost track of what they're looking for. My head is swimmy and tired. I close my eyes and picture Dad. He's wearing cargo shorts, one of the Tommy Bahama T-shirts he used to buy in bulk at Costco. I picture him sitting at a picnic table, alone, a portrait of the county fair we used to frequent when Teddy and I were younger. I picture his hands, but they change quickly, suddenly limp, hardly even wrapped around the steering wheel. I flinch. I picture his body and it presents itself slumped forward like a rag doll. Without thinking, I conjure the sound of blaring car horns, the smell of burnt rubber and smoke. The vision of a cornfield. I open my eyes.

On screen, the Pitbull is still nowhere to be found. The team has spread throughout the forest. I work hard to keep my eyes open and tuck my hands behind my head. I look over at my mother and her eyes are desperate and far away.

"Don't worry," she says, enraptured by the television. "They'll find him."

Dad was killed in a car accident by the Rita's we used to go to for the shaved ice that made my teeth hurt. He was sitting in a line of traffic and a tractor trailer didn't slow down in time.

In the photograph I found in the online paper, his white Toyota Prius looks like a can crunched, accordion-style under a boot. The license plate is blurred for anonymity, but if you look close enough, you can still make out a shred of his old Willie Nelson bumper sticker. Next to the car are two state troopers who look like clones of the same chiseled person scribbling notes. They manage to look both silly and serious in their aviator sunglasses. There is a field next to the road and it rolls forever outward, beautiful in the baking sun.

Haley doesn't think it's a good idea for me to fixate on the photograph. She thinks it will put violent thoughts inside my head. She thinks it's the thing that keeps me up at night. She thinks it's been giving me nightmares.

Mom didn't bother looking at the article, let alone the photograph; she didn't want to see the car. "I know all I need to know," she said. "He's dead, Avery." She said it would be too painful. Teddy didn't want to see it either. It was only me. Now it's something I get to feel alone with. I can't imagine anything more painful than not knowing where and when and how he died. I study the photograph daily, a ritual stored in the pocket of my jeans.

In the morning, Mom invites me to breakfast at the diner and I agree to go. I can't stand the thought of having another meal in the same room as the ashes. It still feels like he's watching me in there, but I also know his eyes are gone. We drive the fifteen minutes to the diner and find a seat between two groups of men from the retirement community just down the road. I slump into the booth and Mom takes the free-standing seat across from me.

"What are you gonna get?" I ask, but Mom doesn't answer, so I peek over the edge of my clunky, laminated menu and her lips are pursed and her face has gotten tense. Her eyes are swimming and they're a touch red. I reach out and place my hand on top of her hand, which is curled on the matte Formica tabletop. And then I return to my own menu.

"I'm gonna get an omelet," I say.

Noisily, Mom clears her throat and I feel her hand slip away from under mine.

"Me too," she says.

When our food comes, we don't bother talking. We eat identical omelets—mushroom and cheese—while I eavesdrop on the table next to us. One of the men is talking about the guttural sound of a mower outside his bedroom window every morning. Another mentions how his wife had left the oven on all night and nearly burned the house down. Another still, mutters something about how weak the coffee is here. They all talk at once; it's like a symphony.

Haley and I have made a habit of listening when we go out to eat. After, we compare stories in the privacy of my bedroom. I try to catch Mom's eye, but she sits and forks through her plate, the slightly bent utensil like a rake to a broken garden. After a while, she leaves to pay the bill up front.

In the car, I thank her for taking me out. She takes my hand and kisses it.

Alex is coming to the house this afternoon to collect the leaves that have piled up around the porch and shred them. This is fall in the woods. Mom has another meeting with the lawyer today, and even though I'm here to be her extra set of ears for things like this while Teddy's away on vacation, I don't want to be a part of it. She drops me home when we're finished with our breakfast and light grocery shopping. To salve the guilt I feel for making her go alone, she leaves me an envelope with a twenty-dollar bill in it for Alex to take when he comes. A task. It feels like I'm back in high school, in need of pizza money while she and Dad go out for a special dinner.

For most of the afternoon, I bum around the house. I drift between rooms. I call Haley, but she's at work; I forgot it was a weekday. My own work at the small newspaper just outside of Boston has mercifully been put on hold or done remotely while I'm out of town and travelling. I sink into the couch and flip through channel after channel, then turn the TV off. I can't stand the noise when it's on, and I can't stand the quiet when it's off. I feel like I'm crawling out of my skin. I go into my parents' bedroom and root through their bedside drawers. In my mother's nightstand, I find: a photograph of Dad on Halloween one year (a bumblebee); a thin, miniature wooden baseball bat Mom's kept in there for years, "for protection"; a tower of vitamins and a bottle of fish oil pills; a box of expired condoms. I shut the drawer.

Alex pulls up around three o'clock in his rust-red pickup truck, and I go out front to meet him with the envelope. Bundles of plastic garbage bags, fat with dead leaves, fill the bed of his truck. He stands next to them in a frayed crewneck sweatshirt—graying stubble, jaw-length black hair, hands tucked deep in his thick canvas pants. He asks me how I'm doing. I shrug and tell him fine.

Alex was the one who called me when it happened, and I screamed when he told me, startling both of us. I could never work out why he was the one to do it. We've been close since I was little, and similar. We're both quiet, a little withdrawn. Alex is like a favorite uncle, a confidante who feels safer and more distant than your parents. And maybe Mom just couldn't break my heart that way. I haven't asked her. I don't know if I ever will. I don't know if I need to know.

I'm a little embarrassed with Alex now, just being around him. He knows what I sound like at my deepest, darkest moment. There's something very revealing about making noise and being heard.

In the driveway, I hand over the envelope. Alex runs the back of his hand across his brow the way I've noticed some men do when they're working and thinking at the same time.

"She doesn't have to pay me," he says.

I shrug and tell him it's only twenty bucks and he smiles.

"The circus is coming to town," he says, lighting a pipe he's smoked for as long as I can remember. His Pennsylvania-southern twang tinges each word as it comes out.

"You don't say." I scuff my shoe across the macadam, booting a stone across the driveway. It narrowly misses pinging his truck.

Alex nods and says, "Yeah, think I might go."

He sits down on the porch stoop and I join him. The smoke smells like bonfire and clove.

The "circus" is what my father always called the Ephrata Fair, a three-day carnival just a town over, complete with rickety roller coasters and cotton candy machines, the works. When Teddy and I were growing up, my parents would take us every year to tire us out after school. Dad always won me a goldfish that usually didn't make it two or three days before floating upside down in the old vase my mother used for its "aquarium."

"What the hell are you gonna do at the circus?" I ask and we both smile.

"I don't know," he says. "Just wander, I guess. Maybe get myself a funnel cake."

"And then what?"

Alex laughs and says, "Nothing, I guess. Go home."

I picture him at home. He lives alone in a small townhouse in Lititz, keeps it meticulously clean, and fosters dogs from the local shelter. Sometimes, when I look at him, it feels like I am looking at some future version of myself. Before I met Haley, our junior year of college, I always pictured myself alone like that.

"Well, I'm not going," I say, picking up a leaf and folding it along the arteries and veins.

"Why not?" he asks. "You're home for it,"

I shift on the stoop. It's unlike him to go for follow-ups.

"Well, I'm twenty-two and childless, for one," I say. "And it just seems—a bit morbid now. Or pointless or something."

My shoulders, where I carry all my tension, slowly relax, the muscles loose and warm in the afternoon sun. Against my nature, it feels good to admit to something private and true. I think of Mom; we've gotten quiet with each other. I'm not sure when that happened, or if it was always the case. Maybe Dad was the thing that bound us all together, our one degree of separation.

Alex shakes his head a little. "Avery, you're gonna blink and this time is gonna be gone from you forever."

"What's that supposed to mean?"

"I mean what you feel right now is gonna go dull," he says, then pulls at the cuff of his sleeve. "All I'm saying is, he might be gone, but he's still fresh. Right now, it's like you could reach out and touch him. It won't be like that forever."

I think of the ashes in the kitchen. I think of the ashes I have back in my apartment up north. Those remains live in a smaller container the size and shape of an egg. My arm itches to move, like I could still reach out and touch him. My dad, still fresh.

Alex runs a hand through his hair. I can tell he's embarrassed for talking so much, so I let my head rest on his shoulder. We sit together for a little while. More leaves fall from the trees, floating and flipping, before touching down in places Alex cleared not half an hour ago. It's sunny, but still cool. It's November. Soon, Thanksgiving will come, and Christmas, and New Year's, and Easter, and Dad's birthday, and my birthday, and in the summer, everything will be wet and hot again; the air will get thick and hard to breathe. Next year, the trees will look just like this but different. I can see it all stretched out ahead of me. It is endless.

The fairground is smaller than I remember it. The Green Dragon roller coaster greets me on arrival, and it too looks smaller and more unstable. Across the way there's a wall of balloons you can throw darts at for prizes. A kid stands up on the counter, flings a dart and *pop*, they got it. A few stands down, a moat of floating rubber ducks.

The noises are nearly unbearable: tinkling funhouse music; shrieking children; announcers calling, *Step right up!* I get in line for a funnel cake next to the lemonade stand, and I buy one for myself. It's a little depressing to realize just how big a funnel cake is, having no one there to share it with. I didn't bother telling Alex I was coming. I had gotten it in my head that I wanted to be alone. Now I'm not so sure. At the end of the month, Haley will come down here with me and we'll bring Juno—because Mom loves Juno—and we'll all eat Tofurkey and watch the Macy's Day Parade. I'll try to show Haley Lancaster and I'll take her to the markets, and hopefully, we'll all be a little less pathetic. I wish I could show her this.

I sit at the end of a picnic table, most of which has already been taken over by a sizeable family. I section the funnel cake into quarters and start eating. Next to me, a German Shephard is sprawled out by its owner's feet, head low and flat on the ground. I drop a little of the funnel cake and scoot it towards the dog with the edge of my boot, until the owner turns around and gives me a look.

To my left, a small boy is crawling underneath the table. He grabs at my ankles before his mother comes and drags him away kicking and screaming. I try to smile at them, but they are already off to the next thing. When I'm done eating, I fold the grease-stained paper plate up thin like a paper airplane and harpoon it into a nearby garbage can. I walk through the maze of vendors and rides with powder sugar dusted on the tips of my fingers and pant leg.

When I make it to the bumper cars, I hear Dad's voice—*That's where I taught you how to drive*—and then the Jack-In-The-Box—*Where you threw up on the woman next to you and I had to buy her a new T-shirt at the merch stand*—and the basketball hoops—*Rigged bullshit. They bend the hoops into ovals!* He saw that on TV once.

There's something a little scary about it, the low grumble of his voice. It manifests itself without effort inside my head. A shock to hear it after all this time, and still, the voice sustains me. I keep walking.

I turn another corner, and more children weave around my legs. Their parents flutter close behind them looking flustered. I'm grateful none of them are mine to worry about and take a deep breath in, as if I can gather all my freedom in my chest and hold it there forever. My mood shifts. After being cooped up all week—inside the house, on the train ride home, even before, holed up inside my bedroom under Juno's soft, vibrating body—there's something calming about being both by myself and surrounded by a crowd of people.

At my urging, Mom is also out tonight; she's with her art group to the movie theatre. It energizes me to think the house, for the first time in a while, is entirely empty. She is not there in the living room, watching dogs on the television, snacking on pretzels and mustard, or dozing on the couch. We are moving through the world again. And he's still fresh; I can hear his voice.

I turn again and find the towering slides and see a bunch of little kids tumble into linen sacks. And then my stomach drops, because right next door, the fish are not where the fish should be. Where there was once an old wooden enclosure, the long folding table with dirty fish bowls and helpless goldfish bubbling for air, now just an empty patch of crabgrass. I walk over to it, slowly, and stand in the void. I close my eyes and imagine the teenage boy—his hair shaggy, his arms gangly and thin—that used to run the goldfish stand. He wore an apron overburdened with singles and five-dollar bills, and a trucker's hat that read simply: *Ephrata!* in loopy cursive lettering. Dad greased his palm one year after spending hours trying to win a fish to no avail. A twenty-dollar bill slid coyly over the counter. We went home with two fish that time, and one of them managed to survive through Christmas, two whole months.

I make my way to the nearest stand—candy apples—and wait for the woman behind the counter to finish with a mid-sized family ahead of me. The mother is holding both her children on literal leashes like they're dogs, and I suppress the first genuine laugh I've had in a while.

"Excuse me," I say, as the dog kids are carted away, caramel-coated apples in their grubby hands.

The woman running the stand has eyebrows plucked beyond repair, but she still raises them when she looks at me. Her fishnet cap is loose around her messy bun.

"Excuse me, where are the fish?"

"What's that?" she says.

"The goldfish," I call out over a swell of music, as a ride behind us takes up again its infinite rotation.

"Oh, they can't do that no more. Animal rights or something."

"But they're goldfish," I say, and it comes out more clipped and condescending than I mean it to.

I look to her for more information. She looks back at me like, do you want an apple or not?

A man is standing next to us and listening, waiting impatiently for his own caramel-coated treat.

"You know," he says, addressing me directly, "goldfish are quite intelligent creatures."

He's wearing a faded navy T-shirt with an eagle on it, a light khaki fishing hat, and his cargo shorts are so low they could be capri pants. Something in me snaps.

"What are you, a fucking goldfish expert?" I say, and he looks taken aback.

"Are you gonna order or not?" the man asks, huffing and offended.

However irrational, I hate him. I hate the look of him. I hate the eagle on his T-shirt, its talons wrapped around a disembodied tree branch. I hate the circus and everyone inside of it. I just want a goldfish.

I turn to the woman and do the only spiteful thing I can think of.

"I'll take all the apples you have," I say.

"You can't buy *all* the apples," the man says.

"Watch me," I mutter, but my cheeks are flushed and hot.

"You want *all* of them?" the woman says, sounding sleepy and annoyed.

Frantically, I fan out some bills—twenty, forty, sixty, eighty—all the cash I found hidden in an old shoebox I used to use for savings as a kid. I slide it all across the counter, knowing what a strange hill I've chosen to die on.

"How many will this get me?"

I have to put the apples in a flimsy cardboard box there are so many of them. I don't even like candy apples, and I feel stupid as I navigate them back out through the circus and into the grassy lot where all the cars are parked. If what they say is true, he must be watching me and laughing.

I weave through the field of cars, the pathways between them so narrow my shoulders keep knocking into rearview mirrors. One mirror, belonging to a particularly high-riding truck, catches the side of my head, and I stumble away swearing. By the time I make it back to the car, I am tired and crabby. I drop the box of apples to the ground. Through the driver's side window, something shiny catches my eye: the car keys, taunting me from the cup holder. I hear his voice again.

What the hell is this? An orchid?

"It's orchard," I say, sliding down to sit in the grass, my shoulders pressed uncomfortably against the door of the car, my head in my hands.

Big difference.

"Actually, it's a really big difference," I snap, pressing my palms hard against my closed eyes. "An orchid is a flower; an orchard is a field of fruit trees," I say.

They both grow in the ground.

I sigh. "Please don't do this."

They are both made up of plants. They both need water and sunlight. For photogenesis.

"It's photosynthesis," I say, almost desperate now.

Jesus, did we raise you to be a snob, or what?

I look up, straight up to the sky. Its depth is washed out by all the lights from the circus, and the stars are far less decipherable than they should be in this secluded county. It's a cliché, I think, to expect something grander from the sky, but I expect it anyway. He's still fresh, and I expect to see his face. I expect to be able to reach out and touch him. I am sitting next to a box of apples I don't want and a car I can't get into, let alone start. And as the aching disappointment settles deep into my chest, the far-off tinkling of fair music worms its way into my ears.

I call my mother.

I was born on a Tuesday in early October, so early in the morning my parents expected me on that Monday. Dad always told the story like it was a sweeping epic. *It was a Tuesday in October and it was dark outside.* It made me giddy to hear him animate the details of my arrival; he always put on his it-was-a-dark-and-stormy-night voice. *Mom and I were huddled close together, hour after hour, and then, boom! You were there too. And everything went calm, and everything was better.* For years, that's how he put me to sleep at night.

A few years after I was born—boom! Just like that—Mom had what my grandpa called "female complications." A botched surgery to remove a cyst that had formed in an ovary left her needing a full-on hysterectomy. She was thirty-two. I was three. Teddy was seven.

We stayed with my grandparents for a week and a half, eating popcorn out of metal tins and slurping SpaghettiO's for lunch and dinner in front of the television. When the time came to leave, I helped my grandpa harvest ripe tomatoes from his home garden to take home. Dad picked us up alone. I wondered where Mom was. Her absence was palpable.

Dad sat me down when Mom first got home from the hospital, just the two of us, and told me her stomach hurt and couldn't hold any more babies. I asked him why and he told me sometimes these things just happened.

Mom was distant for a while. Slowly, she returned.

Throughout my childhood, she took to calling me her girl, my girl, her one and only, a phrase I treated with suspicion even then. I'd survey my favorite toys, a collection of metal cars Dad and I built up over years of going to antique shops down the shore. Which one of them would I be willing to part with? And which would I keep, if I could only ever have one? I wasn't her one and only baby, but I was the last, and there is something to be said for mothers and their daughters.

But it didn't make sense to me to have just one special thing. At night sometimes, I'd wonder what it would be like to have another sibling, a twin, or someone entirely different from Teddy and me. An alien, maybe, like in *E.T.*

I'd picture face after face until the faces didn't look like mine anymore, and there were so many possibilities, and I was just one person.

Mom answers her phone on the second ring, but when I try to speak, I can't.

"Avery? Is everything okay?" Her voice is hushed and hurried. I picture her in the movie theatre, rushing down the darkened aisles. "Avery?"

"Can you come get me?"

"Come get you where?" Her voice is clearer now; she's made it out into the hallway.

"I'm at the circus," I say. "I'm alone."

There is a moment of silence, nothing but the faint hushing sound of our phones connecting to each other. However faint, the noise is soothing and I close my eyes, listening.

"I'm coming to get you," she says. "Stay where you are. I'm gonna come get you."

I wait. I watch the slow trickle of cars, as the lot empties all around me. I pick a few peanuts off one of the caramel apples, but I'm more restless than hungry. When Mom pulls up, I don't recognize her right away. Another woman is driving and it's a car I've never seen before. I watch them pull slowly through the field, and I watch the look on Mom's face change from searching, to concerned, then finally to recognition. When she finds me, her eyes come alive. The woman driving, I can see now, is her friend Mia. She stops the car but stays inside, while Mom gets out and comes to me. I'm still sitting in the grass next to my box of apples. I don't want to move.

"Hey, good lookin'. You need a ride?"

Her humor—something I haven't seen in what feels like a very long time—pulls me apart. I feel like a ball of yarn, once tightly wound, now scrambled in a soft pile. I start crying and make no attempt to stop this time. Mom sits down next to me and wraps her arm around my bony shoulders; I lean into her. I try to take slow, deep breaths. Doing so, I smell faint traces of Clinique Happy, wintergreen gum, and the orange spice tea she drinks with honey.

Finally, I get it out: there weren't any fish.

Mom brushes her fingers through my hair, and we sit until my breathing steadies. My face dries, and my skin is taut and cool. I look over at Mia, who sits unashamedly watching us from her Honda Fiat. Mom follows my gaze.

"Looks like we're better than television," she mutters, and I laugh. She looks pleased with herself. "What's with all the apples?"

"I got into a fight," I confess.

She nods. No other explanation is necessary.

LADIES AND GENTLEMEN

The first man I date is named Lucas, which I think is promising. My cousin was named Lucas. He was a victim of childhood leukemia. He was very small—like a mouse—and loved baseball, and had a rock collection, and he always played as the boot when we pulled out the Monopoly board. The second Lucas I knew was a boy in my high school. This Lucas was gay and didn't know it yet. Everyone else had gotten the idea, which felt cruel so I decided to tell him one day at lunch. *Lucas, you're gay.* He got very angry at me, but years later, he messaged me to tell me I was right. Anyway, I knew it was a good name for boys.

But the Lucas I date is not at all like the other Lucas-es I've known. He does not like baseball and he is not a queer. *So*, I say, *what do you do?* We are in a restaurant that looks fancy from the outside but serves frozen bulk food, all dark wood columns and a sleek central bar and a salad bar for a fixed price. The Lucas I date says he works at a tech startup and goes on to describe work I know nothing about and have no interest in. Soon, he says: *It seems like I'm losing you.* I try to appear more attentive. The booth is tight and lit by a single electronic candle. He talks for two hours. I drink three three-finger whiskeys on the rocks, from the well. Outside, we kiss in front of the restaurant. His lips are too soft, but I accept them. He has a man musk about him. He needs a shave. *My place or yours?*

***

I am dating men this year. Last year, I dated a woman who was like a man in that she had short hair and did not like to clean the apartment. We were together for two years. We broke up on my birthday. She broke up with me on my birthday. And so, I am dating men this year.

I know this sounds misogynistic. That's what my childhood best friend Molly tells me. *Just because Lizzie was a cunt*, she says of my ex, *doesn't mean you get to swear off women*. But honestly, I am sick of vaginas. I tell Molly I need a change, something new. Eventually, Molly tells me she understands, but I know she only says this to make me feel better; we are good at allowing each other to do things we would never even think about doing ourselves.

The second boy I date is named Robert. He looks undeniably like my ex. He has curly wisps of auburn hair and his eyes are a startling shade of green, more sea glass than emerald. I used to think green eyes were a myth, until I met Lizzie. She winked at me the first time we parted ways and it made my stomach jitter. In retrospect, I should have known she would be a total cunt about things. Who winks?

Robert is not a total cunt. Robert is actually quite the gentleman. Molly says the idea of a gentleman is inherently misogynistic—*I don't need a male-bodied person taking care of me and opening my doors*—but I am exhausted by her language sometimes. I like it when I don't have to open doors. Door handles are the dirtiest things in the world, dirtier even—as one study boasts—than toilet seats. Toilet seats, I suppose, are cleaned more frequently. I wonder if Robert knows this, so I tell him.

"Huh," he says.

I nod gravely.

We are in a five-star restaurant eating fancy cheeses that will make my stomach hurt. The waiter comes to pour us both more wine. I gulp mine down. Robert describes his family. He is—obviously, I think—very close to his mother. I tell him the last time I saw my mother we had a screaming match in Macy's over the perfume she wears. I mean it to be a comic story, but it sounds kind of demented as it comes out of my mouth.

Immediately after I stop speaking, Robert continues. He speaks as if he's in the middle of a presentation and needs to make good on time. I eat more cheese. I think about the toilet seats. The more you worry about something being dirty, the more you clean it and the less dirty it is. The only problem is everything else gets absolutely filthy. There are only so many hours in a day.

***

We first met in a book club I joined post-college immediately after I started working a real job in the marketing division of a company that made very expensive running shoes. It was not necessarily a dream of mine, but it paid easily for my studio apartment in Cambridge, where I could walk to local shops and restaurants feeling young and even relatively rich.

In an attempt to feel more grounded in myself, I joined a book club at a local independent shop that ran a few different groups: bestsellers; indie press; horror and true crime. I've never been much of a reader, so I went with indie press figuring it would be chock full of lesbians. Two birds, one stone.

I was right. Lizzie was the book club leader then. She had a charismatic way about her face. She always looked like she was grinning and like it was genuine. Not many people, I thought, can grin and be genuine at the same time. I was impressed by her immediately. She had interesting questions and she would cling to her copies of each book when she spoke, as if she wanted to shake it by the shoulders and ask for all its secrets. She was tall enough and she was butch. This, coupled with her enthusiasm, made me love her.

One night, the two of us hung back from the group and clumsily stacked the folding chairs. As we were finishing up, Lizzie suggested we get a drink together down the road at a little dive bar on Mass Ave. The rest of our small group had already dwindled and dissipated, a few of them meandering back through the shelves to browse or out into the streets, headed home.

"A drink," I said. "Just us?"

Lizzie smiled. There was something sharp in her eye, like a bit of treasure or debris that glints in the underbrush of a well-worn hiking path. I felt myself drawn to her.

"Yeah, just us," she said, smiling in a way that made her seem shy even though I knew she wasn't.

I smiled, too, stacking one chair on top of the other. I didn't know what to say.

"What are you afraid of me or something?" Lizzie asked, which made me laugh, not because it was funny but because it gave me such a funny feeling in my stomach.

When all the chairs were stacked and pressed against the walls, we walked together to a bar I had never been to. It was dark and filthy, and the beer was cheap and cold and good. At the end of the night, Lizzie handed me a book and told me to read it. *The Lover* by Marguerite Duras.

***

Three days after my date with Robert, I meet Molly in a coffee shop that charges money for the internet. We both agree this is old fashioned. A woman next to us interrupts our conversation to inform us it's supposed to help keep the tables open. Molly says she doesn't care, but for some reason, I thank the woman for telling us.

"You say 'thank you' and 'I'm sorry' too much," Molly tells me, when the woman leaves and we're alone again.

"How much is too much?"

"If you have to ask that question, it's too much," she says and reminds me of the time I apologized to a wall for bumping into it.

"I thought it was a person," I say, defending myself.

"You didn't think at all," she says. "You just spoke."

Think before you speak. In the third grade, we learned the word for these sayings: *adage*. I could never pronounce it correctly. *Add-idge. Ah-daj. Add-age.* I don't know how to fit my mouth around these letters; I don't know what's meant to be hard and what's meant to be soft.

"How are the men in your life?" Molly asks and I know she's fighting the urge to make fun of me.

I ignore her and focus on the menu.

"I can't decide what I want," I say.

"Have you been talking to Lizzie?" she asks.

I ignore her again and browse the list of sandwiches.

"What do you want for breakfast?" I ask.

"Eggs with cheese and toast," she says, and it sounds like an incantation.

I leave to order for us at the counter. To our order, I add on two black hot coffees with two packs of Splenda, each, and ask the café worker to give us stirring spoons because we hate it when the sugar clumps to sludge at the bottom.

When our food arrives, we eat. I scoop my eggs onto my toast and make a sandwich. Molly eats everything separately and in a very specific order. I love her for this; she's behaved this way since we were little. Eggs, toast, coffee. When our plates are picked clean, we sip and stir our coffees and talk of little things and television. When we are set to leave, Molly reaches out to me. She takes my hand and squeezes it. I am struck by the softness of her skin.

"Please," she says. "Don't talk to Lizzie anymore."

I don't know how she does this, but she always knows my secret wishes before I do.

A bird in the hand is worth two in the bush. Lizzie was the bird in my hand. She was shorter than me, which was unusual. Usually, the butch one is both taller and more muscular than the long-haired lesbian in the relationship. The butch one also builds the furniture. Lizzie built our furniture, but she was not taller and she was not more muscular than I am. We had an arm-wrestling competition one night and she lost six times in a row. This made me smug and unbearable, she told me. When we played again, I let her win.

Molly is also a butch woman. There must be something about that masculine energy that reels me in. Or maybe, it's the ambiguity. The alluring realization that masculine traits can exist outside of men. There's a kind of freedom in that. There's pain, too.

Butches sometimes don't get along with each other. If masculinity is learned, then so is insecurity. Lizzie was like a man in that she was very insecure and needed constant reassurance. Molly is also insecure, but more so in the way of the generic woman: quietly, privately, morosely. Lizzie was insecure externally. In company, for example, she would bring up novels she had read and mention "films" she had seen in the independent movie theatre. Lizzie refused to go to the normal movie theatre. Whenever I suggested showings at the normal movie theatre, she would remind me that I'm not supposed to use the word "normal" anymore and mutter something about capitalism.

"You sound like Molly sometimes," I joked one afternoon.

But Lizzie didn't like that comparison. Or rather, she didn't like the suggestion that someone I was sleeping with bore resemblance to someone I could be sleeping with and wasn't.

"I'm not attracted to her," I insisted.

"Okay," Lizzie said.

She smiled, and it was a sour smile like clotted milk.

I learned a lot from Lizzie without her ever explicitly teaching me, which is an unsettling feeling. It's like trying to piece a puzzle together when all the pieces are the same shade of pink. I never knew for certain what she wanted from me.

But Lizzie did teach me things. And I did learn. I learned I am very good at listening. I am capable of listening to another person speak for hours without interruption, which counts as stamina. Lizzie taught me I have stamina.

I learned I need to be better at constructive listening, or active listening. *Don't just sit there. Say something.* I learned I like cappuccinos (her drink) and that corn muffins are best served with maple butter (but not too much). I learned it can be difficult for queer women to have friends and date at the same time.

Queer women cannot be friends with other queer women for obvious reasons. They cannot be friends with straight women because straight women will fetishize their sex lives. They cannot be friends with men because: *They'll never treat you as their equal. They'll never take you seriously.*

Lizzie had a very straightforward view of the world, which was comforting at times. Being with her was a bit like giving into an old movie you can never seem to part with, even as it continues to reveal its glaring flaws. I am reminded of the old rom-com rule: men and women can never be friends because sex will always get in the way. Or maybe, it was always the other rule, the more insidious trope: that two people who are very different, who may not even like each other very much, are destined to fall in love for all eternity.

The third man I date is what my mother calls a keeper. He is well groomed. Manicured scruff and gelled hair. Large arms in a tight purple sweater. His boots cost a lot of money and are meant for working physically demanding jobs, but I know the Keeper works inside an office building. He wears a pair of trendy glasses and the lenses are so thin I take them to be fake. I think—I know—he got them at CVS.

The Keeper takes me to a restaurant in the basement of a townhouse. It is dark and you are still allowed to smoke in it. I'm asthmatic but say nothing. Molly would surely scold me for this. *Silence is a betrayal of the self.*

I hold my breath for as long as I can in the smoky basement restaurant. The Keeper goes to the bar. It seems they know him here, because he's greeted immediately with two mixed drinks and he raises them and nods. If money is exchanged for the drinks, I don't see it. I picture him coming back hours later to hastily pay for everything we order. What an odd way to show a woman you are powerful: deferred payment.

When he gets back to the table I am light-headed and breathless from both the smoke and my attempts not to inhale it. When I start breathing heavily, the Keeper must mistake it for attraction, because his foot grazes my leg beneath the table. I squirm but worry he will read any movement as encouragement, so I sit stock still and do my best to breathe normally. The Keeper tells me a jazz band will soon start and asks me if I like jazz. I think, *Does anyone really like jazz?*

The Keeper is the only one I sleep with. In the morning, he gives me coffee, croissants, and orange juice. His apartment looks like a gutted factory: exposed brick, cement floors, bared lightbulbs. I ask him where he found the place and how much he pays for it, thinking it must be a lot. He says it's unromantic to talk about money.

As I leave, I say, "Thanks for the croissant."

Later, I will joke that it was all worth it for the croissant.

A fight. A year ago. We were drinking in our apartment. Lizzie's boxes had yet to be unpacked, and they surrounded us like a fort. There were twinkling Christmas lights strung along the perimeter of the windows. The space felt warm and enclosed. My cheeks were red and Lizzie pressed her fingers up against my skin to cool me.

"How does that feel?" she asked. I said it felt good and smiled. This made her feel good, too. We started playing cards. I won three games.

"Again?" I asked. Enjoying my victory, I shuffled the cards.

Lizzie sipped her drink. "Let's play a different game," she said. I agreed. She explained the game: we'd each reveal something about our past, something we hadn't revealed before, and we would just keep going back and forth.

"Okay," I said, even though it didn't seem like a game to me. "I'm in."

"Okay, I'll start." She cleared her throat.

Lizzie kept a pig as a pet when she was little. I had an aquarium and killed all the fish. Lizzie once found dirty messages on her father's computer. She told no one. I once stole a polished stone from my teacher's desk and it turned out to be a present from her late grandfather. I was in the fourth grade. I kept it because I was terrified of confessing.

"You're a bad person," Lizzie said, but she was laughing.

Lizzie and her friends used to throw pebbles at passing cars. I took a family heirloom and sold it when I was poor in college. Lizzie had a pet snake in college and "lost it" in their apartment. She told her roommate it had died. Molly and I kissed once at a party back in college when we were very, very drunk.

"You told me you weren't attracted to her," Lizzie said.

"I'm not."

"Fuck you," Lizzie said. Her face was taut and ugly like a crumpled sheet of paper. Harsh lines of tension, eyes creased, lips pursed. I became aware of how much we had had to drink.

"Liz," I said.

But Lizzie only stood up, and in a jerky, spastic motion she spat at my feet. Some of the bubbles splattered up onto the wooly fabric of my sock. I was amazed by how little this affected me. The act was so drastic and odd it seemed to level out all emotion. I felt nothing at all.

The fourth man I date is named Henry and I like him very much. He is more relaxed than the others. He takes me to a brewery that is not too packed and not too loud. We are surrounded by groups of friendly strangers. Henry is wearing a simple button-down and a zip-up hoodie. His boots are expensive, but they are worn and he tells me he works construction. He has earned his boots. He is in the union. I find this, for no particular reason, extremely attractive.

I know in the first fifteen minutes that Henry and I will sleep together on the third date like ladies and gentlemen do. Tonight, we will drink three local IPAs each and he will take me to my doorstep and wave from the bottom of my stoop. He is that kind of boy.

At the brewery, we talk in equal measure. I tell him I am from a very small town in Pennsylvania, mostly known for its Amish community. He tells me he's from New York and it has knocked his tolerance for noisy places. He prefers a quieter life now and lives just outside the city. He asks me if I'm Amish. I laugh and tell him no. He laughs and tells me he was only joking. I blush. I am having a good time.

When we are finished with our food and drinks, we split the bill evenly and un-self-consciously. Even Molly would marvel at this man who is not afraid of going Dutch. His appeal starts sinking in. I really like him and this makes me nervous. When he walks me home, I panic and blurt out: I also sleep with women. Henry laughs in a nice way.

"Okay," he says.

"Not in like a fantasy way. Like, in a real way," I tell him.

He smiles. "Yeah, I didn't really think you were offering up a show or anything."

I relax a little. "It never seems like the right time to say it."

He waves me off. "I get it. I mean, I'm sure I don't really. But, it's okay."

Back at my apartment building, half of me wants him to come inside, but I know he won't and the other half of me is thankful for this. I have a quiet, private night ahead of me to think about the possibility of seeing him again. When he leaves, he kisses me on the cheek. Quickly, to catch him last-minute, I kiss his cheek, too. I see him blush and smile, and I know that he's surprised by me. For once, I am satisfied with my first impression.

Inside, I hang my keys on the hook by the door and take my boots off. I sink into my mattress and check my messages. I am married to a landline and an answering machine I keep just by the bed. On the answering machine, I find a message from my mother (*I don't know why you still keep this thing if you never answer....*). There is also a message from the barbershop for Lizzie who used to give my landline out when she didn't want to be bothered. There is also a drunken message from Molly screaming *Call me back you dyke!* And finally, a long, stalling message from Lizzie, the first in months.

I play the message three times over. Each go-around, I have to listen to all the other messages, because I don't quite understand the workings of the answering machine. Slowly, I get more of what she says down on paper. She speaks sometimes quickly, sometimes slowly, which gives the impression of a poem segmented into lines and stanzas at odd parts of every natural phrase. On the third time through, I have the whole message scrawled across a loose sheet of notebook paper:

Hey, look, I'd like to speak with you. I guess—I guess I miss you. Anyway, it would be great to see you. Let me know when we can meet. (Pause) This is Lizzie. K. (Pause) Love you. Bye.

I look down at the paper and shred it.

An hour later, I tape it back together.

At a café that does not charge for Wi-Fi, I play games on my phone and wait. I ignore the texts I get from Molly. Henry texts, too. *I had a really nice time (not in a generic way).* Soon, I am no longer early and Lizzie is late and I start to hate myself.

We've been apart six months now with only sporadic communication: she comes to retrieve a sweater and we have sex in the afternoon (always strange); she texts to say how sorry she is for everything; I text to let her know my uncle passed away; she texts to let me know the panda at the zoo—the one we were both quite bonded to—has died; I text to let her know I'm drinking wine and thinking of her, only her; she texts to let me know she's seeing someone else and hopes, one day, we can be close friends again. Our communication stops until she leaves the message on my answering machine.

When she arrives, the air changes. The boisterous, humming café has lost its sound and movement. Lizzie hovers in the doorway searching for me. I relish the moment. It is like I am watching her on a screen. I am in my living room alone and she is a famous actress in a movie and I have a crush on her. I will watch this scene on repeat for hours on end, savoring the slender, upward trail of her body and the searching movement of her eyes. When she sees me, she smiles with no teeth and gives a small wave. Shy or nonchalant, it's unclear how she is feeling.

"Hey there," she says. Nonchalant, I decide.

I slide her cappuccino across the table, but she tells me she's actually on a caffeine cleanse.

"Oh," I say. Now I will have to drink both cappuccinos and feel sick afterward.

We make small talk. Her eyes are less green than I remember, but maybe it's just a trick of the light—cloudy today, glaring, white-gray. There are many pauses in our conversation. I start wishing Molly would show up to break the ice. *Hey, you fucker. What are you doing back in our life?* I smile at the thought of it.

"What?" Lizzie says. She doesn't miss a thing.

"Oh, nothing. I—"

"Look," she says. "Before you say anything, can we just—can we go out? For a walk. It's too crowded in here and I don't know. It might be nice to move, yeah?"

Her tongue is resting on her lower lip and I can tell she's nervous if not uncomfortable. Her eyes are wide, the irises striking now. She is wearing a hat and it pins her loose curls in such a way that small, exposed wisps frame her face beautifully. And there is something very beautiful about her. Femininely beautiful. It strikes me then, maybe because of all my recent men, that Lizzie is a woman and I love this about her.

"Sure," I say. "Moving sounds good."

We walk for a long enough time that we don't have to think about our legs anymore; they just take us. We are in a part of the city that is grassy and surrounded by little pockets of water. We go in and out of the shade of trees. One minute, we are very cold. The next, we are sun-warm. The sky is clearing up. The day is clear and would be very warm were it not for January.

"So, how's work then?" Lizzie asks.

I start to answer her, but reconsider it. "You don't really care about my work," I say, instead.

Lizzie smiles as if to agree with me, but says, "I do. I'm curious."

"I don't even care too much about my work," I admit.

"Okay, fair," she says. "What have you been reading then?"

I stop, realizing for the first time in months that I am not reading anything at all.

"You've given it up?"

"Only for now," I say stubbornly, as we start walking again, slowly teasing our way around a small lagoon that is filled with geese. "Shouldn't the geese be gone by now?"

"Gone where?" Lizzie asks.

"Gone south," I say.

"They are south," she says. "Those are Canada Geese."

Right, I think, relativity.

"Everything's relative," Lizzie says and I'm annoyed at her for treating me like I'm stupid.

"How've you been?" I ask.

She makes a so-so gesture with her hand. "I'm okay."

"How's your girlfriend? What's she like?"

I can see she never thought I'd be so bold to ask outright. It amuses her the way a precocious child might amuse a therapist.

"We broke up, actually," she says.

"I'm sorry to hear it."

"Are you?" Lizzie says and whips around in front of me.

We are facing each other now and we are no longer walking. I realize we are very close together. Reaching out, I could touch her with my arm still bent at the elbow. I saw a woman the other day. She was walking a dog. At the crosswalk, both of them stopped, and I watched as the woman crowded the dog until it sat down by her feet, a clear understanding between the two of them. I wonder what Lizzie expects me to do with her face so close to mine. Almost immediately, I feel silly for wondering.

I know exactly what she expects of me. It is the same thing I have learned to expect from myself. I will forgive her. I will be happy to hear she is single again. I will connect the dots. A break up. A message on my answering machine. A stroll through the park together. At the end of this, I'll accept a beat-up paperback she's probably stowing in a pocket somewhere, specifically to share with me at the end of our conversation. *Read it, then we can talk about it*. The assurance of a future meeting to "talk about it." If I move forward just a little bit, she'll move that much closer and touch her lips to mine. After, things will go back to how they were. In this moment, I am surer of myself and my instincts than ever. I know I only ever have to wait for her. I know she will always come back to me.

"I'm seeing a man," I say. Lizzie's face splinters like a piece of old wood. "His name is Henry."

"A man," she says.

"Yes," I say and my voice sounds like it is coming out of someone else's body. "I needed a change. Do you know what I mean?"

"No," Lizzie says. "I guess I don't."

I'm surprised by this and say so. "I thought you would, actually. You seem like you need a lot of changes."

"What's that supposed to mean?"

When her nostrils flare, she looks a lot like her father. Stern and Northeastern, like she might be at the helm of a boat off the coast of Cape Cod.

I tell her, "You're not very consistent."

"I follow my heart," she says, defiantly, which I think sounds silly. This makes my whole body vibrate, to think of her as a silly person.

"Other people have feelings," I say, losing control a little and trying not to sound manic. "I have feelings and just because you believe in following your gut or whatever, that doesn't mean you get to ignore everything else that's going on. You don't get to ignore me."

"I'm standing right in front of you," Lizzie says.

"But you don't care how I feel." My lips feel very dry so I lick them. "I really am curious. I don't think you care how I feel. I think you only care about your own feelings."

"What the hell is the matter with you? That's not true."

"You broke up with me on my birthday," I blurt out, feeling like a child.

Lizzie's head snaps backward then forward, a movement that screams. *Jesus Christ, not this again.*

"Even before that, you weren't very nice to me." I surprise myself again. It's like my body has taken hold of my brain, my mouth, my vocal cords. It's barely a choice to speak now, and like the body scabs over aging wounds, I feel very taken care of. Silence, I remind myself, is a betrayal of the Self.

"Well, this was clearly a mistake," Lizzie says.

"I guess it was."

"You're clearly not ready for this."

"Ready for what?"

Lizzie purses her lips, then says, "Real relationships are complicated."

I think, this is toxic. But I tell her I agree, they are complicated, because even now I want to touch her arms and trace the pattern of freckles that spreads across her cheeks.

She looks out on the pool of water and I follow her gaze and we are both quiet and still. Our bodies are just as close as they have always been. This place of not quite touching, of not quite looking at each other, of not quite walking away just yet. There are ripples in the water from the geese and their paddling feet. There are fluffy cattails that round the edges of the water. I think of plucking one and touching the soft top with the pad of my finger.

BAPTISM

We're in Roscoe's beat-up station wagon with the broken AC and Willie Nelson is playing on the radio. Miles back, Roscoe turned the volume up and it's so loud I feel as though Willie's face will soon manifest itself in front of me, all gray goatee, some patterned red bandanna, and skin that looks like sagging leather in a good way. For once, I keep my mouth shut; I don't want to make a fuss. Instead, I look out the window and the trees whip by, their branches smudged by movement. My mother told me once that this was her favorite part of travelling. "Everything is smudgy and soft," she said. "That's a modern kind of beauty, isn't it? It's not like you'd ever go so fast by horse." I thought you could, actually—go so fast on a horse to smudge the things around you—but I liked the way she said it. I kept my mouth shut then, too.

"Pass me a Twizzler," Roscoe says.

I offer up the crinkling bag of Pull-N-Peels and ask him where we're going.

"Surprise," he says. The string of candy swings from his mouth in the middle of a three-lane merge on 222, headed North.

Roscoe bites into his Pull-N-Peel, because I guess he can't pull and peel and drive at the same time. This annoys me for some reason. It's too hot outside and my legs are sticking to the leather seat. The trees are making me nostalgic, so I watch Roscoe instead.

Roscoe looks like a stupid person when he's concentrating, all wide eyes and slack face. His baseball cap is old and faded, more dark-gray than navy now. His T-shirt fits him nicely, although his belly is a little round. His shorts are tight and shorter than I'd wear mine, but he wears them unselfconsciously. He has a beard and I notice a flake of his croissant from breakfast. He has always been a little clumsy.

A sudden warmth swells up inside of me, that deep and desperate kind of caring you can only feel for someone after knowing them through all the stages of their life. The beautiful, the terrible. Ruining everything, "Free Fallin'" comes on the radio. Is there a way to know something so well, so deeply and for so long, that over time you start to hate it? What's that quote? Knowing is a kind of loving.

I prop my feet on the dashboard, where my sneakers leave pale smudges.

Roscoe finishes his Twizzler in three greedy gulps, nearly choking but not quite choking. Annoyed, I pop my shoes off and let them thud to the stained cloth footpad. I fix my eyes on my smudgy little trees.

"Just be patient," he says.

Last summer, Roscoe's little brother drowned in a fishing accident. Roscoe hates fishing, never had the stomach for it. Skewered worms and floppy, fishy bodies. He once cried after stepping on a beetle when we were little, killing it, and we'd had a makeshift funeral underneath a nearby oak tree. His brother Joe on the other hand, he was a natural fisherman, which always sounded strange to me. To me, fishing was a game of luck, like playing War with a deck of cards. All luck aside, Joe regularly brought home big earnings from their annual pilgrimage. There were tensions in the family, especially between the brothers.

Just before the accident, Roscoe was living in D.C. and sleeping with men twice his age and drinking fruity drinks in dingy basements, or so I've been told. Come June, he was determined to make himself a part of something homegrown and masculine. He made it a priority to come home, and the men of the house went fishing. They waded into running water in their matching waist-high rubber boots. Lines cast with the flick of a wrist. Worms, dug up from wet earth and run through by glinting, metal hooks. Cool cans of cheap beer adorned by padded koozies. I imagine it the way you might imagine a Bud Light commercial, that cartoonish brand of manhood sans the topless women.

My imagination of that day is nothing short of dreamlike. Vivid, but strange. Both real and outside of our reality. I can almost smell the plain trickle of river water and feel the wind against my cheeks. I can hear Roscoe's voice on the phone with me, his frantic breathing, his words rushed out like a gush of water run through a broken dam. There had been an accident. A storm had rolled through. The current had picked up. Joe had lost his balance and slipped under. It sounded kind of peaceful when he said it like that, refreshing even. To slip your body through cool water.

But he was a bad swimmer, and he was small. His arms were weak. His frame, too slight.

On the phone, Roscoe asked me what to do and I came up blank. My head was swimming. Sometimes we don't have it in us. To give the things we want to give to other people.

In the car, we cruise passed Philadelphia and are soon back in the fields, heading fast for the border of New Jersey.

"We've been driving forever," I say.

"It's been an hour and a half," Roscoe says, rolling his eyes.

Outside, the sun makes everything orange and warm. The corn is high now and I imagine what it would feel like to get lost in it. In high school, Roscoe and I used to drive out to random corn fields, pull over, then run as fast and as far as we could straight in to the sweltering, leafy rows. It was like we expected to find some sanctimonious pit in the middle, some *Children of the Corn* fantasy or nightmare. Anything, we imagined, would be better than Lancaster. The smell of manure thick in the air. The middle-aged men with tucked-in polo shirts, crimped baseball caps and heavy bumpkin accents. That stiff, slow way of talking. The dead glare in the eyes of girls I found too pretty.

"I hate secrets," I tell him.

Roscoe clicks his tongue and says, "We'll be there soon and then you'll know."

I groan. "Are we going to fucking Six Flags?"

Six Flags. The noise, the crowds, the roar of roller coasters. If I wanted to be around screaming children, I would have them. But Roscoe laughs and says no.

I peel another Twizzler. "Are we going to Trenton?"

"Why would we be going to Trenton?"

"Why are we going anywhere at all?"

"Can you ever just be patient and go along with things?" Roscoe snaps.

I open my mouth to speak, but bite my tongue.

When we were younger, this was easy. Being together felt just as simple as being alone. Now, it sometimes feels as if we are old and haven't aged too well, an old movie that's lost its charm since childhood. We return and return to each other, disappointed each time that we are never quite the same. Or, maybe it's that we never change enough. We find ourselves unwilling to release this lifelong hold. We know each other in a way that feels more real than knowing other people. There is something about time and spending so much of it together.

Looking over, I can see straight through him. He is cool and he's secure, easygoing, happy even. His hands are so placed so casually around the steering wheel. His bright-striped T-shirt and that little pair of shorts. He looks like a gay man in his twenties ready for a time. He wouldn't have worn those shorts in high school, but now he's an age-old bear with charm.

My body feels still. I feel like I can take a step outside of time and see the whole big picture of what's happened to us, and what we are now, and just an inkling of what's to come for us, and maybe this is patience. To be slow, and to pay attention.

Growing up in a small town, everyone thought Roscoe and I might get married. We've been best friends since inception, and, to be fair, we had clung to each other with the ardency of future lovers. But by luck or fate or something bigger with a sense of humor, we both turned out a couple of queers. Roscoe came out to me when he was sixteen, immediately after the two of us had kissed each other for the first time—"to get it over with"—and I had shrugged and said *I'm pretty sure I'm a dyke.* I tried to sound cool in front of him.

"You're absolutely a dyke," he said in a truer nonchalance than I could ever muster.

The cool white of an overhanging street lamp washed over the dark cabin of his father's pickup truck, which we had taken to the fields without permission. It was late and my cheeks had cooled from the afternoon sun.

"You knew?" I asked quietly. I had thought I'd been hiding so well.

Roscoe wrapped his arm around my shoulders. He didn't apologize, because he wasn't sorry. We have always been honest with each other.

"I was waiting for you," he said.

It was strangely romantic. He was waiting for me. I recalled a groom on his wedding day standing at the altar. Cary Grant at the Empire State

Building. We slept that night in the bed of the truck. With the center window open, we listened to the static of the radio. And as we drifted off to sleep, the truck's battery went numb until it died without us knowing it. In the morning, Roscoe's father had to tow us.

The sign at the foot of the drive reads *Lost River Caverns .25 Miles.*

"The caverns?" I say, as Roscoe snakes the station wagon up the long drive to the little shack that looks even smaller than it does in my memory of it. Last time we came here, we were in the third grade on a field trip and I didn't have enough money to buy anything from the gift shop.

"This is it," Roscoe says.

"What are we taking a tour?" I ask.

"Well, yeah," Roscoe says. "They don't really let you in on your own. It's dangerous."

"What are we gonna do? Climb the walls? Murder each other with loose rocks?"

Roscoe cuts the engine in the gravel parking lot. We're at the top of the small hill now that overlooks a ring of trees and, beyond the trees, the same fields we passed through on the highway. To our right is the shack, a paint-chipped little building that is roughly the size and shape of a wealthy child's outdoor cabin. Inside, I know from experience, are countless key-chains and flimsy license plates that say your name on them. Inside, you can buy yourself a coffee mug in the rugged shape of aging rocks.

"Only nerds come here," I say.

Roscoe clicks his tongue at me. "What are you twelve?"

"No, I'm twenty-seven. That's the problem. I'm supposed to go on a guided tour of a cavern?"

"Come on," Roscoe says, unbuckling his seatbelt. "We'll finally get to know the difference between a stalagmite and a stalactite. You've been dying to sort that out for years now."

A week after they found Joe's body, Roscoe asked me to stay the night with him. We slept that night like we were children at a slumber party in a pillow fort in his parents' not-so-finished basement. I told him ghost stories, old tales my mother used to use on Halloween and around the summer fire pit, until we were both too scared to sleep. Our bodies were jumpy and stiff. But soon, we did sleep, wrapped around each other.

When I woke, it was dark and cool. He had said my name, his breath warm and a little wet on the skin. He wrapped his hand around my ribcage and pulled me closer to him. He smelled of his deodorant. Old Spice and a hint of lavender. He smelled of the burnt coffee he'd spilled down his shirt that afternoon. He smelled of the cigarettes we'd shared outside his house, underneath the porch, safely hidden from his mother. The basement was echo-y and strange without the lights on, a kind of cavern in and of itself. Everything felt dank and grim.

We were nestled underneath the staircase in our pile of pillows and blankets, and it became a kind of haven, like the corner of a rug in a game of lava. Roscoe pulled me closer to him still so that our chests were flat against each other and I could almost feel his heartbeat, or maybe I imagined I could feel it. I could hear his ragged breathing, and I could hear my own. My cheek rested on top of his cheek and I could feel the stubble there. His breath was at my ear, and my mouth was close to the nape of his neck.

"What are we gonna do, Natty," he said.

I had no idea. My mother had died of cancer when we were still in college. Losing her had changed the way my body worked. My sense of self. My sense of movement. Time was now a thing that could snap. It didn't just move along like the ticking of a clock. It could jolt out of nowhere, uncontrolled, gone AWOL. The very next moment, it would go back to that same, impossibly slow ticking. For the first three years, I was in a state of vertigo. Dizzy. Distant. Drifting. I didn't know how to comfort other people anymore, so I just held onto him a little tighter.

I had known Joe, of course. His slight frame and calm voice, his smile in the sunlight in the summer. I had known his humor and the slightly tilted gait of his walk. I had seen him play more games of baseball than I had ever cared to see in my entire life. I had seen him lose his temper, only ever when the Pirates lost, his teeth clenched and his lips pursed so tight I thought they'd disappear inside of him. I had known his greatest fears—beautiful women; spiders; the clown at his eighth birthday party. In fact, I had known him his entire life. I had witnessed a beginning, a middle, an end.

The problem with time, when you are grieving, is that there is simply too much of it.

Roscoe cried with me, though his body barely moved. The tears were hot and wetted my thin T-shirt. I leaned in closer.

I tightened my grip on him, hugged him close. Slowly, I reached my hand down and smoothed over his ribcage. When I felt the shine of his athletic shorts, I slid my fingers slowly underneath the slack elastic waist-band. At first, I avoided the front of him, let my hand run the outer flat of his thigh. Soft hairs coated that part of his skin, and I realized he was shaking.

He was familiar because he was Roscoe, but it was very strange to be touching a man that way.

We are adults on a field trip. The same reason I hate going to museums. I always feel so pre-pubescent. But there is, I have to admit, something kind of fantastical about the caverns. They are both comforting and terri-fying. Enclosed, intimate, mysterious. But we are the only adults without children, which makes me feel lopsided and nervous.

The tour guide's name is Stacy and she has the whitest teeth I have ever seen. Her smile dances. One minute she is ecstatic and radiant, the next she has the smile of a psychopath. I feel like I've wandered into somebody else's life and taken up where they've left off. Roscoe avoids all eye contact and nods along to Stacy's presentation. Her voice is clear and strengthened by the echoes of the cave. When she turns to lead us deeper, I pinch the flabby upper part of Roscoe's arm and twist.

"Ouch. What?" he whispers.

"What's up with you," I say quietly.

He looks so genuinely annoyed I want to slap him.

"Come on," I say. "Give it up. What are we actually doing here?"

"We're learning about the caverns."

"No," I say. I latch onto his arm in honest now and hold him back with me from the rest of the group. "What's this about?"

He readjusts his baseball cap and scrunches up his face a little, a ges-ture you might make if your nose is itchy and you can't touch it.

"Are you crying?" I ask. Roscoe shrugs, apparently unable to speak.

There is a fork in the cavern, a decisive left-hand pathway and a mir-rored right-hand pathway. As Stacy and her group of "youngsters" have taken the right-hand pathway, I drag Roscoe to the left and we walk for a little while. My hand is wrapped so tightly around his arm I wonder if I'm afraid to lose him. Like Orpheus and Eurydice, I recall the story in my mother's voice, the light and shadow of her face above a lighted flashlight. Roscoe trails so close behind me and I can't bear to look at him.

When we make it to a bulb-like clearing, the ceiling of the cave gives way to cathedral standards. It's so—cavernous; it's striking. The walls are rugged and cool to the touch. We can hear the sound of trickling water at some unknown distance. We stop and are quiet. We don't look at each other, but rather at this space that holds us.

I point to an icicle-shaped formation hanging from the ceiling, the distant curve above us. "Stalactite," I say quietly, having learned this only moments ago from Stacy.

Roscoe glances upward, then looks down and nods to the ground. "Stalagmite," he says.

The rock formation is like a pointed tooth sprung up from the ground, some demon tooth, larger than an orange pylon and roughly tiered upward to a rounded point. Everything is the color of earth. Brown and reddish. Wet some places, dry in others.

"Stacy would be proud of us," Roscoe says and my laughter echoes back to us.

Roscoe isn't even trying to smile anymore. His expression matches the deeper down part of his eyes, something buried there. Dull.

"Honestly," he says. "I just needed out of that fucking house."

I picture my own house, a cramped studio apartment in downtown Lancaster, so cheap and for a reason. My mattress on the floor. My kitchen like a playhouse kitchen. My bathroom like a cupboard. There are books piled in all corners like some demented library. On the windowsill, a collection of dead plants I have too frequently left without water. Still, there is something home-y about it; it is entirely my own. Roscoe has been staying with his parents.

"How's your mom?" I ask.

Roscoe doesn't answer. Won't, or can't.

"Your dad?"

He shakes his head. He is crying now and I feel a little guilty for making him. The tears roll down his face. One of them slides straight off and slaps against the floor. Perhaps, if we stand here long enough, he will make his very own stalagmite. He'll become a little part of this place.

"Don't make a stalagmite joke," Roscoe says, as if reading my mind. He wipes his face with both his ape-like hands—they are long-fingered and kind of hairy.

"I wasn't gonna make a stalagmite joke," I say, but when he looks at me, he laughs, and the sound is louder than anything we've mustered so far. The sound feels powerful to me. It reminds me we have power.

"Do you wanna scream?" I ask.

"In a cave?"

I look all around the circle of cave. "I think it would feel good."

"You're probably right," Roscoe says.

I tell him I'm always right. He smiles, bites his lip. He looks mischievous, the way he used to look when we were teens and stealing Mountain Dew from Turkey Hill. Our bodies were fresh then. Our minds were sharp and arrogant and dumb.

Should we do it? A silent question. We have gone so long without feeling good.

When we scream, our vocal chords feel like tender strings raked over. The act is jagged and painful and loud. We scream ourselves sore and empty. When we are done, I realize I'm still holding onto his arm, my grip all the more severe with every bellow. This hurts us, too.

When Stacy finds us, we're so swiftly escorted from the cave and into the blaring sun of afternoon. In the cavern shack, they take our photographs and we are smiling. We are never allowed to return.

In the car, we are delighted with ourselves. We feel light. We feel new.

Roscoe stole us both a keychain. For the memory, he says. And we know something we didn't know before: a stalagmite is a formation that arises from the floor of a cave, born from drippings that fall, slow and steady, from the ceiling; a stalactite is something of the opposite.

The clearing is at a concave bend in the Schuylkill River, so the patch of visible water is in the shape of a macaroni. On either end, a cluster of trees so thick and green with summer leaves they don't look real. The grass looks wet and lush, and the dirt beneath is the rich brown of mud. The current is a meager one today. At least, it looks that way. You can't really know until you're in it and you can feel it. My mother used to tell me sacred places are the ones that hold our pain.

The cabin of Roscoe's station wagon feels stale. The sunroof is open and the air is bright and warm above us and around us. The radio is softer now and fuzzy with static so far from the common roads and highway. I can feel the pinprick of early sweat around my shoulders. I feel my cheeks are sunburnt. I feel warm and tacky all over. Mindlessly, I jingle my keychain, my pointer finger placed through the loop so it can dangle.

"You want to go swimming?" Roscoe asks.

I trap the keychain between my fingers, stopping it dead.

"You bring your suit?" I ask.

Roscoe smiles, indulging me. "What about you? Still hiding a one-piece under there?"

For a time, as a child, I had worn a one-piece bathing suit under all of my clothing.

I shake my head and we stay quiet. I am reminded of the night we spent in the bed of his father's truck, and it feels like we are meant to reveal something true about ourselves. But what?

When I heard the news about Joe, I was washed in a strange feeling of calm. I was relieved. I had lost my mother. And now, Roscoe had lost something precious, too. It was a stupid way to think of it, but I had been feeling so alone.

"I let his hand go," Roscoe says, picking at a dry patch of skin on the pad of his palm.

"Hm?"

"Joe," he says. "I let go of his hand."

I shake my head. I tell him Joe slipped. I tell him it was an accident.

But Roscoe isn't looking at me. "I was really scared," he says.

Before he can say anything else, I reach over and take his hand. A bird is cutting circles in the sky above us like a kite. I think of the night we spent in his parents' basement, the two of us moving together, so clumsy and desperate, our touches cloying on the skin. I guess we'd been hoping for something different, something easy and new. Like redemption. We had tried and failed to redeem each other. After, we could barely even look at each other. Eventually, Roscoe asked me to leave. And I did leave. It was cold and close to morning in the pale silver of dawn, and I was grateful to him for letting me go.

Roscoe clears his throat and says, again, "I want to go swimming."

I look out on the water. I note how it moves in waves, one small stream after the other, relentlessly eroding the shoreline.

"Okay," I say. "Let's go then."

The water is cold. It feels good on our tacky skin, as we wade into it. We've abandoned our shoes by the water's edge, and our socks dangle from their open cavities like dead, deflated things. We've stripped our torsos free, my sports bra tight around my ribs. We leave our shorts on. We are like children in the summer.

We hold hands until we make it deep enough where we can no longer feel the smoothed over stones press up against our naked feet. We can no longer stand. I admit the whole thing is a touch baptismal. This could be some backward religious experience. Two queers in Pennsylvania, leading each other to the water.

"It's fucking freezing," Roscoe says, spitting water out and breathing strangely, shaking.

I laugh out loud. I swim.

Ahead of me, Roscoe turns. His body is long and weighty. He turns and floats on his back. There is a trail of hair from his chest to his navel. The sunlight pushes through the trees above us and makes a doily-mark of light and shadow across his face. His skin is beaded with water and it glistens. I stop moving forward. I tread water and watch him drift and sway in the waves. I watch as he closes his eyes, and I wonder what he's thinking of.

I dive beneath the waves. When I resurface, I am next to him.

CLOSING THE DISTANCE

My daughter is working, early, in the yard. I hear her footsteps from my bedroom, my windows overlooking the teardrop of grass and the ring of hostas and ferns, the Japanese maple on the very edge of my property. It's been this way all summer. She's left her job, moved home to be a gardener. My gardener. Soon, her shoveling will start and I will not be able to sleep again. The cleaving: it's too much, too rhythmic. *Thwack, thwack, thwack.* I get up.

Peering out the window, I can see only the back of her: a gray T-shirt sweated through already in the shape of a racer back sports bra; the chicken breast curve of her shoulder blades; the slightly tilted bend of her spine—she has always favored her right for some reason. The nape of her neck is shaved clean; her hair is short. Her legs, bent now as she kneels in fragrant mulch bedding, are muscled and tanned. She wears hiking boots every day. There is a baseball cap resting backwards on her head and I can just make out the knitted design of her old hockey team logo. Underneath: her loose curls—which she gets from me—and underneath those curls she is a mystery.

My daughter quit her job. A good job in the city that paid her well, awarded benefits. My husband and I never thought she would have insurance past the age of twenty-six—she studied writing in college—and then a newspaper of all places gave her a salary, health insurance, paid vacation.

All of that was gone now with the simplest of explanations: *I just couldn't do it anymore.* She showed up two months ago with a duffle bag, a brown, open-faced box, her old Saab parked askew in my driveway. *I just couldn't do it anymore.* I didn't say a word, just opened up the door and let her in. I helped her unpack her things into the spare room, and I didn't say a word.

In the yard, the grass is soft beneath my feet and sinks a little. July has gone muggy with humidity; I understand why she starts her work so early. I just don't understand the work itself. Years of writing late into the night, reading tirelessly through summer vacations, studying the classics, going to some small liberal college up north—my daughter wants to be a landscaper. I suppose there are worse things in the world than a lesbian landscaper.

"Morning," I call, as my daughter's shovel jabs the mulch. She leaves it there, the handle sticking up.

"Oh, hey," she says, turning only slightly before returning to her work.

"What is it today? Morning glories? Geraniums? Little spruce trees?"

My daughter sighs and leaves her shovel in the ground again. "What do you want, Mom?"

"Nothing, nothing," I say, sounding light, I hope. "Just saying hello."

I stand behind her, admiring the Japanese maple. Its bark is shiny in a way that makes me want to slide my fingertips all over it. Its branches are delicate; it is young, new, planted by my daughter just this summer. She says it won't get too much bigger. Still, it will give enough shade to the yard. I hear her grunt a little in the mulch bed; she works herself too hard.

"You need a drink or anything?"

"I'm fine," she says.

"I have iced tea in the fridge, unsweetened. And there's soda in the garage."

"I know," she says. "I'm fine, thanks."

Her arms keep working and I notice she is making a neat little row of identical divots, aesthetically pleasing.

"I can make some coffee," I say.

A forceful sigh, and my daughter plants her shovel yet again in the mulch. "Do you want me to have a coffee with you?"

"Oh, no," I say. "I was just saying. I can brew a pot, if you'll have some, too."

The length of her forearm runs across her forehead, nudging her baseball cap so I can see the light red spots left by the adjustable clasp. She really shouldn't wear it like that.

"There's always the Keurig, too," I say. "If you don't want any, I'll just make a single in the Keurig. It's really no issue."

More digging. There's a small plastic skid of potted flowers sitting next to her, just by her bended knee. Purple, gold, orange. They're beautiful. My daughter wipes her face again, this time with her shirt pulled up and over her face. She rests back on her legs, breathing deeply.

"No, no," she says. "I'll have a coffee."

In the kitchen, my daughter plates our meal with care. Two slices of golden-brown toast with too much butter. The way I like it. Scrambled eggs for her; two eggs, over medium, for my plate. Two links of breakfast sausage—each. My daughter, so meticulous since birth. There is a smudge of dirt left on her cheek, her cheek pink from sun and work. I resist the urge to wipe it with a moist towel. In the cool of the central air, she wears an old hoodie from her high school field hockey team and there are holes in it. I have, too many times, offered to darn them. She has, each time, refused. Mothering, I have learned, is an exercise in restraint.

"Thank you for the breakfast," I say and smile at her. I try not to show just how pleased I am. "It's nice to have you home."

"Well," she says. "It's not forever, but it is nice. Thanks, Mom."

I smile, shift in front of my plate of food. "What should we do?" I ask.

"We should eat," she says simply.

And so, we do. We eat together on the porch. The dog settles in between us on the floor, panting. The dog, a rescue chestnut hound, loves to be outside. His name—enigmatically—is Cartridge, as in ink. We call him Cart. My daughter loves him without borders. She pets his head, caresses his slim face.

"Are you a good boy?" she asks. "Are you a handsome pup?"

I slit each egg with my fork and the yellows ooze out slowly, ever outward. I take up a bit of toast and mop the runny yolk with it. I take a bite: buttery, silky, nourishing. I watch my daughter and the dog. She sneaks him bits of people food, I know. I know she does this, even though I tell her not to. I tell her: *You will make him into a bad dog.* But my daughter's love transcends—she will feed him bits of people food, she will pet his grumbling belly, she will kiss his velvet snout.

Privately, I want this kind of love from her. Her hands in my hair, her devotion. I want her to sneak me private things, small pieces of her meals. I want her to look at me and say, "Aren't you beautiful? Haven't you been good today? Aren't you a good mother?"

"Hey," she says.

I look up, startled. "Huh?"

The look on her face is one of pain, concern.

"What is it? What's wrong?" I ask.

"You're crying," she says, nodding in my direction, gesturing at me.

I brush a hand across my cheek and my fingers come away wet.

"Oh," I say. "Oh, how silly."

I wipe my face with the napkin in my lap. I smile, shrug, as if to suggest the tears are not my own, that I played no part in making them. *Where did these even come from?*

I settle deeper in my wicker porch chair. Smile, always smile. There is a nice breeze now, though the air is getting hotter, heavy as a wetted blanket. I return to my plate. My daughter does the same, eats slowly, in silence. At least, I think, she is feeding me, too.

At night, my daughter insists on sleeping in the upstairs guest room. She needs, she says, to be alone when she sleeps. I wonder at this—is it true? Is she hiding something? Is it me? In bed, I lay awake with Cart. He is thin and chilly in the cool, night air. I wrap my arms around him, but he does not feel satisfying. He is too thin, his ribs showing on the long, curved flat of his side. Still, I consider, in a way he is perfect—he's my dog.

Cart and I found each other in tragic circumstance. My husband had been dead a little over two years (car accident, drunk driver). Still, I was not sleeping well. I was eating almost nothing but peanut butter sandwiches to calm my stomach, not yet for hunger. One morning, the milk in our refrigerator had gone sour and clumped, so sludged and forgotten it brought fresh tears to my eyes. I am now a woman who allows her milk to rot, I thought. I steeled myself. My daughter was not yet home with me. My son, always working, settling down, building a life. Alone, I got in the car. I drove.

On the way to the store, I found an inlet for distraught vehicles and pulled over. I looked out. We live in a county so sparse and fielded it appears, at first glance, abandoned. Were it not for dots along the horizon—a far-off tractor tilling in the field; a silo filled with wheat; the single light gone on at dusk in a distant farmhouse—one might imagine this place a rolling expanse of emptiness.

On the side of the road, I looked out and saw nothing but the cropped stalks of corn, their color waning from true green to an unattractive grayish brown. Slowly, my eyes dried. At the sight of it all, I felt the size and weight of myself. These fields. Their width and breadth enveloped me; the color, washed of vibrancy, soothed my shaking hands; I became calm. In the distance, I saw a man and a dog trotting through the field. The man wore a rigidly brimmed straw hat, a solid purple button down, simple black pants—Amish. The dog, I could tell, was young. They were not working. They were out and enjoying each other's company. And they were the only living things that marked the land.

I did not buy milk but kept on driving. Cartridge was the only dog left at the animal shelter. He came home with a leash and a thin winter dog jacket. Love is so easy to give to something that will surely love you back. That first night we played fetch all through the house with a pair of my husband's old socks. I don't think he would have minded.

I wrap my arms tighter around Cart's body. He fidgets only once, then gives into my embrace. I picture my husband. Tall, rounded in the middle, like a baby whale made vertical, given legs to walk on. His hazel eyes and the soft red of his cheeks after a glass of wine with dinner. His hands, so large and decisive—tugging at my sleeve to get my attention, like a boy in the supermarket with his mother. His feet spread outward, flat and smooth—he had slipped so many times on our new hardwood floors. His shorts: cargo. His T-shirts: pocketed, Costco brand. His lips—they are my daughter's lips. Teddy looks like me, but my daughter. She is the two of us all mixed up together. I hug Cart tighter. He is asleep already. We are, I remind myself, two living things that mark this space. Together, in my king-sized marriage bed, we sleep.

It is not the shovel but the mower that wakes me in the morning. It is so early my head hurts, protesting consciousness. Cart is curled under the covers; he will not budge. Reluctantly, I swing my legs over the edge of the bed. I stretch, arms up and over my head. I yawn, eyes watering, spit sprayed. My feet just graze the floor and it is cold. Outside, I can see the sky is candy blue and wisps of cloud drift in and out of view. The edges of the neighbors' trees border my window. Leaning forward, I see her: my daughter, expertly operating the old hand mower she revived on her return.

I grumble down the stairs. I put the coffee on to brew. I check the dishwasher—I forgot to run it the night before. I purse my lips, roll my neck—remember to breathe. I breathe. I turn it on and go out on the porch where I can watch my daughter, her arms like chicken wings pushing the mower back and forth all through the yard. When she was little, my husband killed a cluster of baby rabbits this way. My daughter had cried for weeks after that. He had cried too, privately, only to me. He was soft, like a tender peach ripe for picking. But to our daughter, he showed only his solid, sturdy pit; he never wanted to bother her, never wanted to upset her with his sadness, his grief, his guilty feelings. Over time, I noticed she took to this, too, not allowing him to see her cry, only ever showing him a happy face, a playful nudge against his body. A couple of beers cracked open on the porch. Pistachios shelled for each other and popped, salty and dry into the mouth. They laughed a lot.

"Hey," I call out, waving my arm to get her attention. She is wearing his old ear muffs. "Hey!"

Her face flickers. She looks around, then sees me standing there. A single finger raised: *Hold on a second.* I sit down on the porch steps and stretch my legs out so my feet rest in the freshly cut lawn. The sun feels good so early in the morning. I let it soak my skin. I close my eyes. I am almost asleep again by the time I hear the mower sputter to a stop. I open my eyes to see my daughter—sweaty arms bared by her rolled-up T-shirt sleeves, the flush of her cheeks (so like his cheeks), the bouncing gait of her stride. She takes the ear muffs off and lets them hang from the back of her neck.

"What's up?" she asks.

"It's seven o'clock in the morning," I say. "Did you have to mow the lawn?"

"It needed it," is all she says, shrugging a little. *What's the big deal?*

I look up at her. She doesn't quite meet my gaze. Seven years on and there is still something dull in her expression. She is half dead or half stranger. She is not the lively self of yore—food fights in the kitchen baking Christmas cookies; heated arguments over the dinner table; the fire in her belly just after finishing a good book. *You have to read this; now, now, now.* She used to shove our hands full of battered paperbacks.

I slap my hands down on my legs and push myself up standing. "Okay," I say. "Sorry, okay. Do you want breakfast?"

She looks at me, but this time I deny her eye contact. "Sure," she says and drops her work gloves to the grass, wipes her sweaty hands down the front of her shorts.

We go inside. I open up the fridge. I will make her breakfast today.

My daughter will eat my food in my house. She will be the daughter. I will be the mother.

"What's the plan today?" I ask.

My daughter sits at the counter and swivels on a bar stool, still panting from the work. "Not much, actually," she says.

This is a turn. I extract the eggs from the fridge and start cracking them into a bowl. Usually, my daughter has a list a mile long of what she'll do, excuses, I'm sure, should I ask her to do something with me. We live again in the same house, but there is distance. It is very hard to lose a parent young in life. I read that sometimes, children will turn sour, subconsciously blame the living parent for being alive.

"What are you up to?" my daughter asks, sipping orange juice.

Where did she get orange juice?

"Oh, nothing," I say. "Just, hanging around. I'll walk the dog later if it isn't too hot on the paws."

My daughter chokes on her juice, then, with cup removed from her mouth, I see she is actually laughing.

"What?" I ask, hesitant, unsure if I'm allowed to laugh, too.

"I don't know," she says, coughing, smiling. "'Hot on the paws.' Made me laugh."

"Well, I don't know why. The pavement can burn the shit out dogs. You have to be careful."

"I know," she says, and she pulls at the back of her neck, stretching. "It just sounded funny, okay?"

She has that look about her, the one resembling exhaustion—is she exhausted with me?

"It is kind of funny," I say, in a sore attempt to save something happy between us.

We don't talk about my husband anymore. We hardly talk about anything.

"I'm gonna go shower," she says. "I'll be down for breakfast, all right?"

She pecks me on the cheek, strides down the hallway; I hear her bounding up the stairs. And just like that she leaves me feeling like a failure, as if something I caught has been taken from me, as if an award has been stripped from my neck. Empty. I feel empty.

I whisk the eggs. They spit hot oil in the pan.

At the dog park, my daughter chats with the owner of a Boston Terrier, a man in his mid-thirties. I wonder if she is flirting. She wears loose-fitting cut-off canvas pants, hiking boots, that damn field hockey hoodie. On her head: the baseball cap. She looks like a lesbian. To me, she looks like herself, but when I push myself outside of being her mother, she looks so obviously like a lesbian it seems her whole aesthetic must be very carefully constructed and impossible to miss. It's a little embarrassing.

But the owner of the Boston Terrier—bearded, broad-shouldered, taller-than-her—seems so intrigued their interaction cannot possibly be platonic, can it? I keep an eye on them. Could she, after all these years, be interested in a man? And what would that mean for us? I correct myself— for me. What would I do with a straight daughter? A vision of manicures and pedicures, a wedding in a church, a house with a yard and hedges, grandchildren. Grandchildren that look like us, like me. I turn to my side out of habit, but there is no one there next to me and it feels like I've missed a step going down the stairs. I clear my throat, turn back to look ahead.

And just like that, Cart is nipping at a German Shepherd; they don't know when to stop. I call my daughter over to help us tear the dogs apart. The owner of the Boston Terrier hovers close behind the mess, guarding his own dog and still feeling some need to engage with the situation. But my daughter doesn't hesitate. She struggles in between the dogs, stumbling as their bodies swirl around her legs, fingering Cart's collar. In the process of separation, her hand gets bit. Not badly, but there is a little blood. She tugs Cart roughly by his collar and clips him to his leash in one fluid motion. I am astounded by her, this master wrangler before me. Somehow, I can never shake the feeling of my daughter as a child; she's still so young.

"Are you okay?" I ask.

She sucks fresh blood from the wound on her hand and I wince.

"It's fine," she says. "It's okay, but we should go." She turns from me to face the dog. "Come on, Carty," she says, patting his sun-warm ribcage. Her tone is soft with him.

I swallow hard and follow them.

In the car, I hold myself in. I am driving, steady and strong. I want to ask my daughter how she's feeling. I want to ask if she is okay, but worry she will only snap at me. On her hand, the bite is turning black and blue. I want to ask so many things. There is a silent waterfall between us made of questions.

Do you need money? How long will you stay with me? Why did you leave that job? Why did you run from the city? Was it the girl? The one you were seeing with the nose ring? Did she break your heart? Is your heart still broken? Are you missing your father? How often do you think of him? And what do you feel when you think of him? And is it strange for you to be here with me, only me? As it is strange for me to be here with you, only you? And where do you keep your urn and do you ever hold it? And did you love him more than you love me? Do you still love him more than you love me?

I settle at a red light. My daughter sighs. Cart is stretched across the seat behind us. The air is so impossibly still. The radio is on and quietly humming something I don't know. My daughter lifts her feet to rest on the dashboard, leaving marks there. I say nothing, even though I've told her not to do that many times. When the light turns green, I pull forward and think sometimes his death has cheated me. The suddenness of it has made it nearly inconsolable, as if we may never recover. It is so drastic a change. I do, I admit, feel cheated. Not merely by the loss of it myself. I feel cheated, too, by the way it has changed my child, how the loss has taken her from me. How she no longer thinks of me the way she used to. How she no longer sees me. My daughter, she is here with me. But she is guarded now, and strange. I want to shake her. I may not be the one she is looking for, but I am the only one she has left. I feel, far more intensely now, the way I felt when she spoke her first words: *Dada*, instead of *Mama*. My husband, I remember, had gloated.

"How's your hand?" I ask to break the silence.

"It's okay," she says.

"Liar."

She sighs. "It hurts."

"We should—"

"I'm not going to a doctor."

My lips purse. Why are young people so averse to going to the doctor?

"Were you flirting with that man back there?" I ask, changing the subject.

"What," she says, half laughing.

"It just looked like you two might be getting along."

"I wasn't flirting," she says firmly.

"You were smiling a lot."

"We were getting along. We were talking about dogs."

"It looked like you were flirting."

My daughter adjusts herself in her seat. At first, I think she might crawl into the back to get away from me. She seems genuinely annoyed now. Why can't I ever let anything go?

"I don't mind that you were flirting, you know." I adjust my grip on the steering wheel and signal a left-hand turn. "It's okay with me, if you—you know, many people date both genders."

"Jesus Christ." My daughter wraps her hand in tissues from the center console. "I wasn't flirting with him. Full stop. Can we please stop talking about this?"

"Can I ask you a question?"

"Well, you are on a roll right now," she says.

I eat the pain she causes me. I ask, "How are you?"

"What?"

"I mean, really. How are you, really?"

The car is making a funny sound I have to call about. I will not bring it to the dealer this time. In my widowhood, I have learned the hard way. Too expensive. I turn again onto a road near home. We make it through a second light.

"Bad," my daughter says, simply. The word is easy and redeeming as an exhale.

At our road, it occurs to me that in the car we cannot escape each other, so I keep driving.

"I'm bad, too," I say.

"I know," she says.

"You know?"

"Of course, I know," she says and still, I wonder how. My daughter settles deeper into the passenger seat, her feet propped again on the dash. She hugs her knees closer to her chest. "I worry about you," she says.

I keep on driving.

I want to tell her she doesn't have to worry about me, but it feels like something too many people have said before. So much so that I end up saying nothing more at all. Instead, I keep on driving. Actions speak louder than words. Right now, I think, I am speaking with my actions: As long as I keep driving, that's how long I want to be close to you, trapped with you. We are in the fields again. The fields, they soothe. Perhaps, I think, this is the reason for all her gardening. All that dirt under her fingernails. It's like balm to a burn.

"Where are we going?" my daughter asks.

"I didn't know you worried about me," I say.

Her hand slides across the top spread of my back, the part that doesn't quite touch down against the seat when I am sitting up and focused. A warm orange light spreads in through the windows, the sun a lowering blaze in the sky, the colors softer now like the smudges of an oil painting. My daughter's palm, calloused from her working in the yard, slips from my back and her hands return to her lap. She starts picking at the callouses, and I want to tell her to stop that because it's really not good for the skin, to be picked at.

At a fork in the road, I take the left-hand branch and the road carves a smooth slight curve through the sheep fields and we enter a one-lane covered bridge. It is dark inside the bridge, and you're supposed to make a wish in the very middle of it.

My daughter says, "I worry all the time."

It's the middle of the night. I wake up and realize I still have hours of sleep ahead of me. And yet, I am awake. Cart is curled against my legs. He will not budge. I extend my arm to the still-made side of the bed and feel like a widow in a movie. I think: my person is gone.

Quietly, I make my way down the hallway to the guest room. The floorboards creak a little under foot, but I leave the lights off. If only I can look at her, I'll be able to sleep again. At her bedroom door, I pause, lower the handle slowly, then push the door forward ever-so-slightly. It swings inward without complaint, no creaks, not a sound. It is a little frightening, actually, to know how easily and quietly someone could open this door. Would an intruder even wake us? I shiver. I enter the room on soft feet. If only to look at her.

But there is no one in the bed.

Thwack, thwack, thwack.

I hear the shovel.

"What the hell are you doing?"

My daughter is crouched in the bed of mulch that lines the edges of the yard. The yard, two months into her stay, is unrecognizable. Small flowers now line the curved edge of mulch. The green of the hostas and the ferns are black in the night, though some are illuminated by the moonlight, a glowing gray. The star-shaped leaves of the Japanese maple cut dark shadows over the lawn. The grass is pristine, soft and buoyant.

It is beautiful. In the middle of it all, my daughter crouches digging. She stops at my voice.

"Jesus fuck, you scared the hell out of me," she says.

"It's the middle of the night," I snap. "What is this?"

"I couldn't sleep," she says, as if this answer is sufficient.

I gape at her. "Warm milk. Honey and tea. Television. Heating pads. Those things help you sleep. This?" I almost shriek the word, gesturing wildly to the lawn that is no longer my dopey little lawn, the simple one that came with this suburban house. "This is insane."

"It helps me," she says.

"Helps you what? Forget about Dad? Work through your shit? Get over the career you threw away? This isn't you. This—this is insane. I can't do it anymore. I can't watch you do this."

My daughter takes a deep breath, releases it so slowly. She gets up and turns from me, strides back into the dark.

"Where are you going?"

"Just a minute," she says.

I hear her crunch through sticks, dirt, gravel. She wraps around the house, disappearing for a moment. Then suddenly, she re-emerges holding a small potted something. As she draws closer, I see it for what it is: a little tree in a small ceramic pot. She comes much closer to me than I expected her to, so much so I nearly back away. She seems, in that moment, unrecognizable, as if I don't know her at all. And then, I look at her: her eyes are my eyes, her lips his lips. Her ears are entirely her own: big but soft, a little pointed. She makes that odd, half-smile expression of hers, and she is my daughter again. She has a farmer's tan. I can see it even in the dark, just above her T-shirt sleeves. I shiver, thinking of the sun.

"It's—here. Just take it," she says, handing me the pot, this small, particular tree.

The truth is that it is not quite a tree yet. It looks, to me, more like a single branch sprouted from the soil. Its trunk is curved like a snake and its leaves emerge in periodic clusters all along the irregular squiggle of "trunk." In its meandering, it is both long and relatively squat. The leaves catch my eye more than anything, so dark in the night they must be vibrantly green. The whole thing is roughly the height of stepping stool you might use to reach the sugar in the kitchen.

My daughter pulls at the back of her neck. Her eyes are fixed on the tree with such deep care it disarms me. Has she really gone insane? I have allowed her to stay here, indulged her garden—have I enabled this insanity? Have I been missing the signs of breakdown?

"Explain," I say. "I don't get it."

"It's called a bio urn," she says, but her words are lost on me. "I took a small portion of—the remains," she says, uncertain of herself. Her words are labored, as if she does not quite know how to speak. Finally, she says, "I made you a tree."

The two of us are quiet but for breathing.

"You made me a tree."

She nods. We look at each other, directly at each other. Together, we return our steady gaze to the tree between us. I am holding a pot. Inside the pot there is soil and through the soil weave roots and from the roots this beautiful, delicate tree that holds small pieces of my husband's body. I think but do not say: it is a little bit like he's alive again. I am starting to understand. I am cool in my summer pajamas.

"I like working with my hands," she says, breaking the silence. "It helps me. I miss him."

I think of sitting in my living room, the couch sagged on each end—mine and his. The empty place, the dent on his side of the armrest from where he pushed himself up each night for bed. It was too much, all that space. I got a dog to fill it in. My daughter built a garden.

My daughter clears her throat, sighs. She shifts in her old hiking boots.

"If you don't like it, I can't take it back," she says.

Surprising myself, I laugh. I am in awe of her. Looking down, I see the ground is dug up in the middle of her garden.

"Is it ready?"

She wipes her face on the shoulder of her T-shirt. She is still looking at the tree. Then, she crouches to the hole, rounding it one last time with her dirty hands. I see only the back of her. Her shoulders are wide and strong. Her curls are untamed and bounce with her movements. She is taller than me now, which is strange—when your children surpass you—but kneeling there in the garden, she still looks very small to me. There is a childlike wonder to her. There is energy in her body. She moves quickly, her movements forceful, and it strikes me that she looks a little angry. I understand this. Who knew anger could make something beautiful?

"Okay," she says, pushing herself up. "It's ready."

She takes the tree from me and I feel hollow in its absence, like I could shatter at the slightest touch. And I watch as her hands work, carefully extracting it from the pot. She places it with the diligence of a new parent lowering a baby to a crib. When the tree is settled, she swaddles it in wet dirt and covers the patch with mulch. She stands and we admire her work.

I can't stop looking at the tree, my present.

"Was it always for me?" I ask.

"I told you. I worry." She smacks her hand against her filthy shorts to get some of the dirt off. "Thought it might keep you company."

Reaching down, I touch the tree for the first time. It's a little rough. Carefully, I pluck a single leaf and hand it to my daughter. She takes it and places it in her pocket.

"You want some tea?" I ask.

My daughter smiles, rolls her eyes. "Okay," she says. "Okay."

Time, I learn, is endless. Time, I learn, is very close so you cannot see it. And then one day, something will wrench you backward. Everything unseen comes into focus. There it is, you think, this thing we call time. It is wide and flat and persistent as the fields. It is unmoving, and still, it moves. *Tick, tick, tick.* It is regular and strict, but it still manages to fluctuate. The darkness comes at four p.m. all winter; the wash of sun at ten p.m. all summer. It is marked and felt differently depending on the person, and yet, we are all beholden to it.

I lay in my bed after the planting and my daughter—the smell of musty dirt and the sweetness of the sweat dried on her skin—lies next to me and sleeps. Cart is curled so tightly by her feet. The sun is coming up outside my window, that pale orange light against the wall. Another day, another morning. I count my breaths, and they come in and out, slow, unending. I fit my fingers in the notches of my ribs.

I have marked my time in varied units: how long has it been since we lost him? How long has my daughter chosen to be here with me, next to me, breathing slowly, too? How many meals have I eaten alone in this house made strange in his absence? How many sleeps with the dog in my bed?

I will mark my years with my husband tree. Every summer, I will measure him. I will count the curves in his trunk. I will survey each cluster of leafy greens, the waxy pads of green pinched lightly in between my fingers. And every week, I will prune his branches. I will give water to his soil. I will view him through the kitchen window, where, if I am so inclined, I might speak to him while I am doing the dishes.

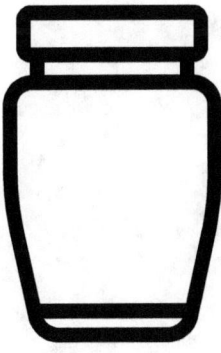

ACKNOWLEDGMENTS

I want to thank the entire team at Split/Lip Press for seeing something special in my work, for believing in it, and for ushering these stories into the world so beautifully. A special thank you to my editor, Pedro Ramírez, for his kind words, thoughtful questions, and the care and generosity he put into bringing this manuscript over the finish line.

Thank you to the early readers of these stories: Madeline Sneed, Will Gibbons, Khánh San Pham, Laura Rosenthal, Mako Yoshikawa, Julia Glass, Maria Flook, and many others at Emerson College. A special thanks to Madeline, for bopping me on the head when I need it and wagging your finger at me when I am doubting my own worth. To Will, for sharing your love of movies and comedy, and for making me appreciate the little things more deeply. To Mako, for reading countless drafts of these stories and for helping me find the joy in it all. And thank you to The Tam on Tremont St. for supplying countless Blue Moons (with oranges) to sustain us all in our writing and friendships.

I want to thank my wife, Jess, for marrying me and for loving me and for making me laugh. Thank you for asking me out via Facebook in 2015. I'm very happy I said yes.

Thank you to my brother Jordan for taking my phone calls, sending me music, and showing me that it really is worth it to make something and to try to make it beautiful.

Thank you to my mom for putting up with my present-day antics and my childhood tantrums, and for indulging my love of menswear from an early age. You've given us everything.

Lastly, I would like to thank my dad, Ernie, who was killed in a car accident on October 4, 2017. He did not understand what it meant when I told him I wanted to be a writer, but he asked a lot of questions and he listened and he tried. I miss him every day. He will not get to read these stories, but he is in them and they were always written for him.

GRATITUDES

"My Share of the Body" was first published in *Pigeon Pages* as "A Share of the Body"

"Baptism" was first published in *Ninth Letter* as "Swimming"

"Closing the Distance" was first published in *Appalachian Review* as "The Husband Tree"

Thank you to the readers and editors who have supported my work and writing. And thank you to the other literary journals and magazines who have welcomed me into their pages: *Passengers Journal, Foglifter Journal, Alien Magazine*, and *The Maine Review*.

DEVON CAPIZZI is a writer living in Boston, MA. Their work has been supported by the Bread Loaf Writers' Conference, the Tin House Workshop, and a fellowship from Emerson College. Their writing has appeared or will appear in *Pigeon Pages*, *Ninth Letter*, *Foglifter Journal*, *Passengers Journal*, *Alien Magazine* and elsewhere. When they are not writing, they are probably cooking. They are originally from Lititz, Pennsylvania.

NOW AVAILABLE FROM
SPLIT/LIP PRESS

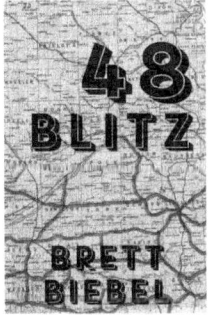

For more info about the press and titles, visit us at
www.splitlippress.com

Follow us on Instagram and Twitter: @splitlippress

www.ingramcontent.com/pod-product-compliance
Lightning Source LLC
Chambersburg PA
CBHW051515260626
47162CB00008B/2974